fiction
12 pts

Siddhartha

DOVER · THRIFT · EDITIONS

Siddhartha

Hermann Hesse

Translation, Introduction, and Glossary of Indian Terms by
STANLEY APPELBAUM

DOVER PUBLICATIONS, INC.
Mineola, New York

DOVER THRIFT EDITIONS

GENERAL EDITOR: PAUL NEGRI
EDITOR OF THIS VOLUME: KATHY CASEY

Bibliographical Note

This Dover edition, first published in 1999, is an unabridged republication of Stanley Appelbaum's new English translation of the work originally published in German by S. Fischer, Berlin, in 1922. The translation, along with the Introduction and Glossary of Indian Terms written by Stanley Appelbaum, was first published by Dover Publications in 1998. An introductory Note has been prepared specially for this edition.

Library of Congress Cataloging-in-Publication Data

Hesse, Hermann, 1877–1962.
    [Siddhartha. English]
    Siddhartha / Hermann Hesse ; translation, introduction, and glossary of Indian terms by Stanley Appelbaum.
        p.   cm. — (Dover thrift editions)
    ISBN 0-486-40653-9
    I. Appelbaum, Stanley. II. Title. III. Series.
PT2617.E85S513   1999
833'.912—dc21
                                      98-31818
                                          CIP

Manufactured in the United States of America
Dover Publications, Inc., 31 East 2nd Street, Mineola, N.Y. 11501

Note

SINCE THE first English translation of *Siddhartha* (1951), entire generations of students in the English-speaking world, and many others who appreciate philosophy expressed in literature, have read Hesse's story of a man who, from his earliest youth, quests variously for *nirvana*, full understanding and development of his self, and the peace of a perfected being. Stanley Appelbaum's new translation of this poetic, beloved novel will engage new generations with this timeless tale.

The title character, Siddhartha, has the same personal name as the historical Buddha, Siddhartha Gautama. As a young man, after spending three years with a band of wandering ascetics, Siddhartha encounters the Buddha, his older contemporary. The youth perceives the greatness of the Buddha's thought and of his way of living, though he cannot accept the teacher's philosophy as a guide for his own life.

Leaving the Buddha and his multitude of monk followers, the young man sets out to seek truth, wisdom, and the way to perfected being— on his own, without following any doctrine or prescribed technique. During the course of his life, a variety of experiences, lived to the full, shape his perceptions. *Siddhartha* reflects its author's thoughts and beliefs about the oneness of all elements of the universe, the meaning of time, the nature of self, and the significance of human beings' loving attachments to others.

Contents

INTRODUCTION

The Author

HERMANN HESSE was born in 1877 in Calw, in the Black Forest region of southwestern Germany. Calw was a center of missionary publishing to which his father, a North German, had been posted after becoming ill while a missionary in India. In Calw the author's father married the daughter of his superior, a prominent linguist; she herself had been born in India when her father was a missionary there. Thus, young Hermann grew up in an atmosphere that was unusually cultured and cosmopolitan for a small town.

But it was also an atmosphere of piety and duty; the boy was expected to become a minister. Although extremely bright, however, and gifted at writing and drawing, Hermann was surprisingly rebellious and difficult. His school record was not brilliant, and, finally, at the age of fifteen, he even ran away from his seminary. A breakdown ensued, the beginning of a lifelong series of visits to sanatoria, spas, and psychiatrists. Formal schooling, and with it a career in the clergy, was eventually called off, and Hesse thenceforth educated himself on his own time—but so successfully that he became one of the best-read of all German writers, and was able to publish a famous reading list of "best books" for people aspiring to culture.

After uncongenial work in a church-clock factory, he concentrated on learning the bookseller's trade, which he had looked into earlier. After four years with a book dealer in the tradition-rich university town of Tübingen, a period in which he began writing seriously, he joined another firm in Basel, and from then on usually resided in Switzerland, although he did not change his citizenship until 1924. In 1899, the year of the move to Basel, his first book was published: *Romantische Lieder*, a book of verse. Hesse continued to write verse all his Life, becoming one of the most prolific and respected German poets of the century. His poems were to appeal to a number of major song composers; three of Richard Strauss's famous Four Last Songs are to texts by Hesse.

Hesse's novels, however, are undoubtedly his best work (although eventually he was also to write many, many volumes' worth of short stories, travel accounts, essays, book reviews, translations, introductions to new editions of classics, articles for periodicals, and a vast correspondence). His first novel, the important *Peter Camenzind* of 1903, was a breakthrough for Hesse in several ways: it began his association with the great Berlin publisher S. [Samuel] Fischer; it brought him enough money and fame to live off his writings from then on, giving up bookselling; and this financial stability allowed him to marry. His first wife, older than he, was to present him with three sons; unfortunately, she was neurotically reclusive, and he was compelled to divorce her in 1923. From 1904 to 1912 they lived on a farm near Lake Constance; farm life was one of several dreams that went sour on Hesse when put into practice.

Another dream that failed to stand up to reality was Hesse's quest in 1911 for some sort of roots in India, a country where both of his parents had lived and whose literature, religions, and philosophies were dear to him. The steamer he sailed on touched at ports in Ceylon, the Malayan island of Penang, Singapore, and Sumatra. Hesse suffered from the heat and from dysentery. He was away only a few months and never set foot in what we call India; English-language reference books that speak of a stay in India are carelessly mistranslating the German word *Indien,* which can also be an overall term covering *Vorderindien* (Hither India; i.e., our "India") and *Hinterindien* (Farther India; i.e., Southeast Asia). Hesse himself referred to his destination variously as *Indien,* Asia, or Malaya. On his return he expressed disappointment, claiming that colonial rule had denatured the territory; he seems to have been more comfortable with the Chinese merchants he met than with the largely impoverished Hindu and Muslim population. (For Hesse's literary works involving India, see the section "The Novel," below.)

From 1912 to 1919 Hesse lived in Berne. Unable to serve in the First World War because of his bad eyes, he worked for organizations that supplied reading matter to German prisoners of war. Though not a militant pacifist, he had pacifist leanings and thus became associated with the like-minded French author Romain Rolland, to whom he would later dedicate Part One of *Siddhartha.*

Hesse had been writing excellent novels and stories all this time, but his real blossoming out came after the war. In 1919 he published pseudonymously (fooling all but a few canny readers) the novel some critics believe to be his best, *Demian* (actually written in 1917). Always concerned with the problems of children and young people (and later encouraged in this by his psychoanalytic sessions with Jung), from *Demian* on he became a recognized mentor of German intellectual and avant-garde youth. During the same year, 1919, he wrote some major short stories, began writing *Siddhartha* (not published until 1922; see "The Novel," below), and moved to the Ticino, the Italian-speaking part of Switzerland. From 1919 to 1931 he rented a villa in the village of Montagnola, near Lugano; it was there that he wrote his weirdest and most experimental novel, *Der Steppenwolf* (1927). In 1931 a wealthy patron built a new, isolated house for Hesse in the same village and gave him free use of it for his lifetime. There the writer lived happily with his third wife (they married in 1931; Hesse's unsuccessful second marriage in 1924 had been extremely brief); he happily tended an extensive garden, received visits from friends and admirers, and continued his writing career.

In the early years of the Nazi Reich, Hesse spoke out against Swiss intolerance toward the numerous German emigrants seeking refuge in his adopted country. Even during the Second World War, however, he still tried to get his new works published in Germany, and he gave hospitality to German writers who had stayed at home. The great product of those years was his long novel *Das Glasperlenspiel* (*The Glass Bead Game*, a.k.a. *Magister Ludi*), published in Zurich in 1943 (the composition had taken eleven years). Although some critics prefer *Demian*, *Siddhartha*, *Der Steppenwolf*, or the 1930 novel *Narziss und Goldmund*, there is no doubt that *Das Glasperlenspiel* is Hesse's most ambitious work, in construction, in imagination, and in style, the one with most breadth, depth, and scope. It was largely on the basis of that novel that Hesse was awarded the Nobel Prize in literature in 1946 (his friend Thomas Mann, the laureate in 1929, had already been canvassing for him for years).

Das Glasperlenspiel was the last major work. Active to the end, though suffering from leukemia, Hesse died of a cerebral hemorrhage in 1962.

The Novel

Part One of *Siddhartha* was written in the fall and winter of 1919. Then, after that amazingly productive year, Hesse experienced a lengthy fit of depression and was unable to continue for a year and a half. He was finally able to finish the book in the spring of 1922, and it was published by S. Fischer, Berlin, later that year. (Various sections of Part One had already been published in several magazines and

newspapers.) Part One was originally dedicated to Romain Rolland;
Part Two, to Wilhelm Gundert, a cousin of Hesse's on his mother's
side, an expert on Japan whose visit had helped clarify the author's
thoughts about Part Two.[1] In a 1950 reprinting, Hesse dropped these
dedications, substituting one to his third wife, Ninon Dolbin.

In German editions, the novel (sometimes called a novella) carries
the subtitle *Eine indische Dichtung* (*An Indian Literary Work*). Though
this can also mean "a work about India," the connotation "a work orig-
inating in India" is strong. This connotation is consonant with the
book's style, which simulates that of an old pious legend. Hesse's style,
although generally lucid and classical, avoiding syntactic or other ex-
tremes, was nevertheless very malleable and could change drastically to
suit varied narrative situations (it should be recalled that almost no one
identified him as the author of *Demian*, although he had been an established author for twenty years). For *Siddhartha* he chose a highly
poetic style reminiscent of ancient scriptures, particularly the sermons
attributed to the Buddha (available to him in excellent German translations), with their parallelism of simple clauses and their incantatory
repetitions. He uses a number of archaic words, unusual forms, and
rarer secondary meanings of everyday words. (This style is imitated in
the present translation, not by using archaisms, but by retaining the
repetitions, avoiding contractions, using "dignified" word choices, and
very occasionally wrenching the syntax where the German does this
very conspicuously.)

Hesse's relationship to India through his family has already been
mentioned, as has his journey to Southeast Asia. *Siddhartha* was the
most important product of that relationship, but far from the only one.
In 1913, for example, Hesse had published the volume *Aus Indien*,
which consisted chiefly of an account of his trip, but also included,
among other items, the short story "Robert Aghion," about a young missionary in India who balks at becoming part of the colonial establish-
ment and who loses his calling when no longer convinced that the
religion he came to impose was necessarily superior to that of the local
population. Another journey to the East, although this time very un-
realistic and much more of a fantasy than even in *Siddhartha,* is the
basis of Hesse's important novella of 1931 *Die Morgenlandfahrt* (*The
Journey to the Orient*). And, significantly, one of the previous incarnations of the hero of *Das Glasperlenspiel* takes place in ancient India.

---

[1] Although the novel is formally divided into these two parts, it actually falls naturally
into three parts of four chapters each. One ingenious critic laboriously attempted to
equate the four chapters of Part One with the Four Great Truths of Buddhism, and the
eight chapters of Part Two with the Buddhist Eightfold Path!

In *Siddhartha* the historical situation is very specific. The sixty or so years of the hero's life can be dated to around 540 to 480 B.C. on the basis of the traditional dates for the Buddha (roughly 560 to 480). This was a period of great intellectual and spiritual upheaval. The older Vedic religion, or Brahmanism, which, at least as far as written records show, was based on strict ritual observances in the worship of old Indo-European deities—observances requiring the participation of the Brahmans, the highest, priestly caste—was coming to an end. The new Vedic writings of the time were the Upanishads, which reinterpreted the religion philosophically and mystically, preaching the oneness of the universe. Brahmanism was slowly developing into Hinduism, which was still polytheistic, but largely characterized by almost exclusive devotion to a single supreme god chosen from among a small number; the most popular gods now proved to be the gods of the common people, who had played only a minor role in the Vedas, Shiva and Vishnu (Vishnu also being worshipped in various of his incarnations, especially Rama and Krishna).

Another contemporary result of the fundamental questioning of the established religion at this time was a number of sects or heresies, particularly Buddhism, which looked on earthly life as mere suffering and whose adherents sought release from the eternal round of reincarnation that was universally believed in at the time. Whereas the Hindu hoped that good works in this life would lead to a loftier and more comfortable position in his next existence, the Buddhist saw no good in living at all, and sought total extinction (*nirvana*). The historical Buddha, Siddhartha[2] Gautama of the Sakya clan, preached Four Great Truths: all existence is suffering; suffering is caused by desires; to stop suffering, one must cease to desire; this is achieved by the Eightfold Path. That path consisted of: correct opinions, correct thoughts, correct speech, correct actions, correct way of living, correct effort, correct attention, and correct concentration.

This original (or "primitive") Buddhism, specifically intended to save those who took a vow of poverty and became monks, renouncing all worldly ties, ignored the gods and included little in the way of worship; it has been called a philosophy or a therapy rather than a religion.

---

[2] It is hard to say why Hesse gave his hero the same given name as the Buddha's (the Buddha is never called by that name in the book); it is a source of confusion at first for anyone familiar with Buddhism—and Hesse expected some familiarity, because he uses a number of Buddhist terms and concepts without further explanation. The similarity of names certainly confused the writer of the short article on Hesse in a prominent encyclopedia; one edition after another has transmitted the notion that the novel is about the early life of the Buddha. (It is rather unnerving to reflect that the author of the article obviously never read the book!)

Much later, however, by the beginning of the Christian era, Buddhism developed in India into the Mahayana ("great vehicle") school, which became a religion for the masses, with an extensive pantheon, a multiplicity of Buddhas, the possibility of instant salvation without great efforts, and an active corps of "guardian angels" (bodhisattvas). In this form, Buddhism (which was to disappear in India) conquered Tibet, China, Mongolia, Korea, Japan, and Vietnam. A form of Buddhism closer to the original survives only in Sri Lanka, Myanmar (Burma), Thailand, Cambodia, and Laos. (For the technical Indian terms in the novel, as well as a brief analysis of the names of the characters, see the Glossary that follows this Introduction.)

Hesse was interested in Chinese philosophy, as well, and even stated that Taoism was a greater influence on *Siddhartha* than Indian philosophies were. Some typical Taoist elements are the praise of quietism, seclusion, and an austerely simple life-style; and the belief that softness is stronger than hardness.

Almost all of Hesse's novels are philosophical and allegorical to some extent; they are not character studies, like Stendhal's, for instance; or depictions of society, like Balzac's; or vivid tableaux of real people interacting with one another and with their circumstances, like Tolstoy's. But *Siddhartha* is by far the most schematic; the incidents can readily be plotted on a graph, and the characters have no more individuality than those in such medieval allegories as *The Romance of the Rose*. *Siddhartha* is a long preachment, quite literally offering us "books in the running brooks, / Sermons in stones, and good in everything." The philosophy, however, is much more emotional and imagistic than systematic or really thought out.

The novel's vitality and connection to reality are due to its genuine sources in Hesse's own life. Siddhartha (minus, perhaps, some of the virtues he acquires at the end, such as unstinting love) *is* Hesse. The struggles of Siddhartha against his priestly father, and those of his own son against him, reflect Hesse's defiance of authority as a child. Siddhartha's conclusion that teachings are useless reflects Hesse's interrupted schooling and his pride in his self-education. Siddhartha's self-doubts and attempt at suicide have real echoes in Hesse's life. Even small details are relevant: the raft Siddhartha builds with Vasudeva may very well refer to Hesse's rides on loggers' rafts when a boy in Calw. Like Peter Camenzind, like Demian, like the *Steppenwolf*, like the Magister Ludi, Siddhartha is an outsider choosing his own path, no matter how disturbing it may be to society (although a fundamentally antisocial life-style, such as a criminal's, is rarely a choice for Hesse's heroes).

Aside from its verbal charm, the book is also enlivened by a series of remarkably insightful touches with a ring of psychological veracity, as when the love-starved Siddhartha dreams he is embracing his friend Govinda and the figure dissolves into that of a nurturing woman.

The book was immediately successful in Germany, and is still regarded by some as Hesse's greatest; there is a vast body of critical literature in German concerning it. It was translated into Hungarian in 1923; into Russian in 1924; into French and Japanese in 1925; into Dutch in 1928; into Polish in 1932; and into Czech in 1935. Translations into two dozen other languages, including over a dozen spoken in India, date from after the Second World War. It was Henry Miller, another kind of influential outsider, who, becoming enamored of the novel, urged his publishers, New Directions, to commission an English translation. Although this pioneering effort, first published in 1951, did not meet high standards of accuracy, completeness, fidelity to the tone of the original, or even proper English, it did yeoman service in introducing *Siddhartha* to the English-speaking world. This novel has remained Hesse's most popular in the United States.

It must remain a matter of personal opinion whether the best possible use was made of the novel in the first decade or two after its English translation; that is, whether Hesse had ever envisioned the book as a side dish to LSD, a hippie handbook, or a bible for the dropout and the draft dodger. Although the unguarded and unqualified terms in which he sometimes praises the rejection of conventional wisdom and morality, inviting the reader to "do his own thing," make him partly responsible for any results whatsoever, only a hasty, superficial reading could have produced the most unfortunate results that did ensue (in some people's opinion).

Today, in a substantially calmer period, we can recognize that this outcry against oppressive social forces, this plea for self-fulfillment despite the expectations of others, was that of a mature, responsible man; a friend of writers, composers, and artists (himself a violinist and painter, as well); a highly educated and sophisticated intellectual aristocrat—and that it was intended for his peers.

GLOSSARY OF INDIAN TERMS

Preliminary Remarks

The lore of Buddhism in India has been chiefly handed down in two different languages: Sanskrit (Saṁskṛta), a direct outgrowth of the Vedic language, and the classical language of Hindu India par excellence (like Latin for medieval and Renaissance Europe; it is mainly the later, Mahāyāna, Buddhist writings that use a form of Sanskrit), and Pali (Pāli), a later, but closely related, language exhibiting significant phonetic simplification vis-à-vis Sanskrit. Pali is the chief language in which the oldest Buddhist writings have come down to us and is the sacred tongue of the conservative Theravādin sect of Buddhism still prevalent in Sri Lanka, Myanmar (Burma), Thailand, Cambodia, and Laos. (See the discussion of Buddhism in the Introduction.)

Hesse, though a voracious reader deeply imbued with Asian thought, was not a scholar, and in this novel he indiscriminately mixed Sanskrit and Pali terms (as well as nomenclature from different periods); in fact, some commentators on *Siddhartha* have seen him as basically a namedropper. Moreover, he never used any of the standard diacritical marks (such as a horizontal rule [or a circumflex] over vowels to indicate length, a dot beneath certain consonants to indicate their pronunciation with the tongue tip placed behind the upper teeth ridge, etc.). Quite naturally, for a few words he used a German spelling that has become standard (just as we do, for example, with "Upanishad"): "Nirwana," "Vischnu," "Krischna," etc.

In the present translation, to avoid confusion and pedantry, the English uses a Pali form where the German does, and a Sanskrit form where the German does; at the request of the publisher, the translation (like the Introduction) also omits the (really useful, if not essential) diacritical marks (the ignorance of which, as well as general linguistic carelessness, has led a few commentators on *Siddhartha* into ludicrous errors). Here and there, it would have been foolish not to use a few standard English spellings, analogous to the German ones mentioned at the end of the foregoing paragraph.

This glossary, however, *does* use a scholarly transliteration, including diacritical marks, and, where necessary, distinguishes Pali from Sanskrit terms. All the terms and proper names are historical and not invented by Hesse, except those preceded by an asterisk (*), which are those of his fictional characters. Two terms in the glossary are not from the text itself, but from the translator's footnotes; they are preceded by a dagger (†).

Agni. God of fire and burnt offerings in the Vedic and Brahmanic religion.

Anāthapiṇḍika. Rich banker who bought the park Jetavana and donated it to the Buddha.

Atharva Veda. The Veda principally concerned with magic spells. See "Vedas."

Ātman. The self; one's own nature; the individual soul. In some of the Upanishads, this is equated with the *Brahman*, or universal soul. The term is Sanskrit, the Pali equivalent being *attan*.

Bo tree. The tree (in Buddhagayā [Bodh Gaya]) beneath which the Buddha was sitting when he attained enlightenment (*bodhi*). It was a pipal, or sacred fig, tree (*Ficus religiosa*). The specific form *bo* is neither Sanskrit nor Pali, but Sinhalese (Ceylonese).

"Brahma, Brahman." For the purposes of the novel, three terms have to be distinguished: (1) Brahmā is either the supreme god, or one of the three supreme gods, of the Brahmanic/Hindu tradition (the creator of the world; in the novel he is alluded to only twice, and the other two terms are far more significant); (2) *Brahman* (a neuter noun) is the absolute, the world soul, the highest being, the unifying principle of the universe (always italicized in the present English translation); (3) "Brahman" (*brāhmaṇa*) is a member of the highest caste, the priests, who guard the Vedic tradition and officiate at numerous rites and sacrifices (this term appears in German as "der Brahmane," in the present translation as "Brahman"; the alternate English spelling "Brahmin" is now chiefly used figuratively and pejoratively). (In this entry, to avoid counterproductive complications, some niceties of Sanskrit linguistics have been intentionally overlooked.)

Chandogya Upanishad. In Sanskrit, *Chāndogya Upaniṣad* ("the Upanishad concerning the chanter of the *Sāma* melodies"), this Upanishad (see that term) is part of the *Sāma Veda* (see that term). Among its chief topics are the mystical meanings of certain sounds, especially the syllable *om* (see that term), and the oneness of the individual and world souls.

Gotama. This is the Pali form equivalent to the Sanskrit Gautama. It was the family name of the man who became the Buddha (see Introduction).

*Govinda. Siddhārtha's boyhood friend in the novel. Hesse probably derived the name from later literature about Krishna (see that entry), where it is a title of Krishna, and sometimes of Vishnu (see that entry), of whom Krishna is considered an avatar (incarnation). The name appears to mean "cow-seeker," and is appropriate to Krishna's life as a herdsman.

Jetavana. A park ("[Prince] Jeta's forest") in Sāvatthi (see that entry), donated to the Buddha by Anāthapiṇḍika (see that entry), who bought it at a vast price from Jeta.

*Kamalā. A courtesan loved by Siddhārtha in the novel. The name means "lotus blossom." The first *a* is short, and the word has nothing to do with *kāma* (love, desire, passion) despite the opinion of careless commentators. That Hesse himself knew what the name meant is indicated, if not proved, by the reference to a lotus blossom in the poem that Siddhārtha addresses to the courtesan; whether even Hesse connected it with *kāma*, as well, is hard to say. Kamalā is also a title of the goddess Lakṣmī.

†*Kāmasūtra*. "Treatise on Love"; written in the early centuries of the Christian era, thus hundreds of years after the events of the novel (although its teachings may have been common knowledge at an earlier date).

*Kamaswami. In the novel, a merchant who takes Siddhārtha in as his assistant. Hesse probably invented the name, which is seemingly compounded of *kāma* (love, desire, passion) and *svāmin* (owner of, master of).

Krishna (Kṛṣṇa). As referred to in the novel, a Hindu herdsman-god of northern India, considered to be an avatar (incarnation) of the major god Vishnu. (Krishna is also a character in the epic poem *Mahābhārata*, in which he utters the sublime *Bhagavadgītā*.)

Lakshmi (Lakṣmī). A goddess, the consort of the great Hindu god Vishnu (Viṣṇu).

Magadha. A large region, part of the present-day Indian state of Bihār. Gayā, where Gautama became the Buddha, was a district within Magadha.

Māra. A demon who unsuccessfully assailed Gautama with magical illusions during the *bo*-tree meditations that led to Gautama's Buddhahood.

Māyā. Illusion; used in different contexts—for instance, the illusion that what our senses perceive is reality; the Buddha strove to dispel illusion.

Nirvana. In Sanskrit, *nirvāṇa*; in Pali, *nibbānaṃ*. Literally, "extinction, blowing out." Used to refer to a death no longer subject to rebirths; the goal of the original Buddhists.

Om (also, *aum*). The untranslatable syllable uttered before every recitation from the Vedas. This prominence led mystics, in the Upanishads and elsewhere, to elevate *om* to the greatest heights — indeed, to the position of the Supreme in the universe.

†**Parinirvāṇa.** "Ultimate extinction"; a term applied to the death of the Buddha.

Prajāpati. "Lord of engendered beings"; an abstract creator divinity often mentioned in the Upanishads.

Rig Veda (*Ṛg-Veda*). The most famous Veda, an anthology of hymns to the gods to be performed at sacrifices.

Śākya. The clan to which Gautama's family belonged.

Śākyamuni. The wise man (or, seer; or, ascetic) of the Śākya clan; a title of the Buddha.

Samana. In Pali, *samaṇa*; in Sanskrit, *śramaṇa*. In general, a wandering ascetic; this is how the word is used through most of the novel. But, in Buddhism in particular, it refers to a mendicant monk, and Hesse uses it in this way at times. From the root *śram-*, indicating heavy labor and exhaustion; some commentators have given incredibly fanciful etymologies. (This term is intentionally not italicized in the translation, since it is such an integral part of the narrative.)

Sāma Veda. The Veda concerned with the chanting of the ritual hymns; it includes some musical notation.

Saṃsāra. Only in the final chapter does Hesse use this term in its primary meaning of reincarnation, the round of rebirths from which Buddhists wished to escape. Everywhere else, he uses it in the secondary sense of "this world we live in, in which we are subject to reincarnation." In this usage, it is reminiscent of *karma* (the actions that inevitably lead to reincarnation), a term that Hesse never uses in the novel. Generally speaking, *saṃsāra* is largely secularized in *Siddhartha*, at times practically reduced to "the annoyances (or monotony) of life."

Satyam (Sanskrit; in Pali, *saccaṃ*). The truth (both literally and as a philosophical principle).

Sāvatthi (Pali; in Sanskrit, *Śrāvastī*). A city in the Kosala region, northwest of Magadha (in the present state of Uttar Pradesh). Location of Jetavana (see that term). Hesse's form "Savathi" is incorrect in any language.

*Siddhārtha.** Hesse's hero, "one who has achieved his goal" in Sanskrit (in Pali, Siddhattha). This was also the personal name of the man who became the Buddha (see the Introduction for a discussion of Hesse's unusual choice of this very name).

Upanishads (Upaniṣad). The most recent writings within each Veda (see "Vedas"); mystical and/or philosophical reflections on elements in the Vedas (or on religion in general). Influential in all later Indian thought and, eventually, on European thought. Some of the Upanishads are gems of literature as well.

*Vasudeva. The ferryman in the novel. The name was probably borrowed by Hesse from that of the foster father of the herdsman-god Krishna in later mythology (see "Krishna").

Vedas. The basic holy books of Brahmanism and Hinduism, probably composed gradually between about 1500 and 500 B.C. The four Vedas are the *Rig* (*Ṛg*) *Veda* (ritual hymns), the *Sāma Veda* (instructions on chanting the hymns), the *Yajur Veda* (a collection of ritual formulas), and the *Atharva Veda* (a collection of magic spells). In addition to the fundamental elements briefly characterized in the foregoing sentence, the Vedas also contain a vast amount of supplementary material, both mythological and theological, including the mystical and philosophical Upanishads (see that entry).

Vishnu (Viṣṇu). A relatively minor god in Vedic times, Vishnu ultimately became one of the chief gods of India, not only in the "trinity" Brahma-Vishnu-Shiva (Śiva), but also—for many millions—the supreme, practically the only, god (but one with many manifestations or incarnations, the two most famous being Krishna and Rāma).

Yoga Veda. There is no such thing, strictly speaking, but there is a group of Upanishads known as Yoga Upanishads, and there is a *Yogasūtra*. Yoga, of course, is the special set of methods of concentration and meditation intended to result in enlightenment or the acquisition of supernatural powers; it is present in some form in almost every area of Indian religion. (Could Hesse have been thinking of the *Yajur Veda?*)

PART ONE

The Son of the Brahman

In the shadow of the house, in the sunshine of the riverbank by the boats, in the shadow of the *sal*-tree forest,[1] in the shadow of the fig tree, Siddhartha[2] grew up, the handsome son of the Brahman,[2] the young falcon, together with Govinda his friend, the Brahman's son. Sunshine tanned his fair shoulders at the riverbank, when he bathed, during the holy ablutions, during the holy sacrifices. Shadow flowed into his dark eyes in the mango grove, during his boyish games, while his mother sang, during the holy sacrifices, when he was taught by his father, the learned man, when he conversed with the sages. For some time now, Siddhartha had taken part in the conversations of the sages, had practiced oratorical contests with Govinda, had practiced with Govinda the art of contemplation, the duty of total concentration. He already understood how to utter the *om* silently, that word of words, how to utter it silently into himself as he inhaled, how to utter it silently forth from himself as he exhaled, his psychic powers concentrated, his brow encircled with the glow of the clear-thinking mind. He already understood how to recognize *Atman* within his being, indestructible, at one with the universe.

Joy leapt in his father's heart at that son, so quick to learn, so eager for knowledge; he saw a great sage and priest developing in him, a prince among the Brahmans.

Bliss leapt in his mother's bosom whenever she saw him, when she

---

[1] A timber tree (*Shorea robusta*) with wood nearly as hard as teak. Buddha was born while his mother clutched a *sal* tree.

[2] Siddhartha; Brahman: see the Glossary for all proper names and Indian terms. The English translation basically uses the linguistic versions chosen by Hesse; diacritical marks appear only in the Glossary (see explanations there).

saw him walking, sitting down, and standing up, Siddhartha the strong, the handsome, walking on slender legs, greeting her with perfect propriety.

Love stirred in the hearts of the young Brahman daughters whenever Siddhartha passed through the lanes of the town, with his gleaming brow, with his kingly eyes, with his narrow hips.

But, more than by all of these, he was loved by Govinda his friend, the Brahman's son. He loved Siddhartha's eyes and pleasant voice, he loved his gait and the perfect propriety of his movements, he loved everything Siddhartha did and said; and, above all, he loved his intelligence, his lofty and fiery thoughts, his burning will, his high vocation. Govinda knew: this man will not become any ordinary Brahman, no lazy functionary at sacrifices, no avaricious merchant of magic charms, no vain, empty speechmaker, no malicious, crafty priest, but also no kindly, stupid sheep in the flock of the multitude. No, and he, too, Govinda, did not wish to become one of those, a Brahman like ten thousand others. He wanted to follow Siddhartha, the loved one, the splendid one. And if Siddhartha should ever become a god,[3] if he should ever enter the company of the Radiant Ones, then Govinda wished to follow him, as his friend, as his companion, as his servant, as his spear bearer, his shadow.

Thus did everyone love Siddhartha. He gave joy to all, he was a pleasure to all.

But he, Siddhartha, did not give himself joy, he was no pleasure to himself. Strolling on the pinkish walks of the fig orchard, sitting in the bluish shade of the grove of contemplation, washing his limbs in the daily expiatory bath, sacrificing in the deep shade of the mango forest, with gestures of perfect propriety, loved by all, the joy of all, nevertheless he bore no joy in his heart. Dreams came to him, and uneasy thoughts, flowing to him from the water of the river, sparkling from the night stars, molten in the rays of the sun; dreams came to him, and restlessness of the soul, smoking to him out of the sacrifices, uttered from the verses of the *Rig Veda*, trickling from the teachings of the old Brahmans.

Siddhartha had begun to nurture dissatisfaction within himself. He had begun to feel that his father's love, and his mother's love, and also the love of his friend Govinda, would not always and for all time make him happy, content him, sate him, suffice him. He had begun to foresee that his venerable father and his other teachers, that the Brahman sages, had already imparted to him the greatest part and the best part of

---

[3] Presumably, in a future reincarnation, as a reward for his exemplary mortal life.

their wisdom, that they had already poured their abundance into his expectant vessel; and the vessel was not full, his mind was not satisfied, his soul was not at ease, his heart was not contented. The ablutions were good, but they were water, they did not wash away sin, they did not heal the mind's thirst, they did not dispel the heart's anguish. Excellent were the sacrifices and the invocation of the gods—but was that everything? Did the sacrifices offer happiness? And what was all that talk about the gods? Was it really Prajapati who had created the world? Was it not the *Atman*, He, the Only One, the All-One?[4] Were not the gods beings that had been formed, created just as you and I, subject to time, mortal? And so, was it good, was it correct, was it a meaningful and supreme activity, to sacrifice to the gods? To whom else should one sacrifice, to whom else was reverence to be offered, but to Him, the Only One, the *Atman*? And where was *Atman* to be found, where did He dwell, where did His eternal heart beat, where else but in one's own self, deep within oneself, in that indestructible something that each man bore inside him? But where, where was this self, this innermost thing, this ultimate thing? It was not flesh and bone, it was not thought or consciousness: thus the sages taught. Where, where then was it? To reach that far, to attain the ego, the self, the *Atman*—was there another path that was profitably to be sought? Ah! But no one pointed out that path, no one knew it, not his father, not his teachers or the sages, not the holy sacrificial chants! They knew everything, the Brahmans and their sacred books; they knew everything, they had troubled their minds over everything, and more than everything: the creation of the world, the origin of speech, of food, of inhalation, of exhalation, the categories of the senses, the exploits of the gods—they knew an infinite amount—but was it of any value to know all this when they did not know the one and only thing, the most important thing, the only important thing?

To be sure, many verses of the sacred books, especially in the Upanishads of the *Sama Veda*, spoke of this innermost, ultimate thing—splendid verses. "Your soul is the whole world" was written there, and it was written there that in sleep, in deep sleep, men entered their innermost being and dwelt in the *Atman*. Marvelous wisdom was contained in those verses, all the knowledge of the greatest sages was gathered together there in magical words, pure as honey gathered by bees. No, one should not hold lightly the immense store of knowledge that had been gathered and preserved there by countless generations of

---

[4] An untranslatable word play on *all* (everything, universe), *ein* (one), and *allein* (alone, unique).

Brahman sages.—But where were those Brahmans, where were those priests, where were those sages or penitents, who had succeeded not merely in knowing this most profound knowledge, but in living it? Where was the expert who could magically transfer his sojourn in the *Atman* from the sleeping to the waking state, to real life, to every step he took, to words and deeds? Siddhartha knew many venerable Brahmans, his father especially: a pure man, a learned man, a man most highly to be revered. His father was admirable; his demeanor was calm and noble, his life pure, his words wise; subtle and noble thoughts resided in his brow—but even he, who knew so much, did he, then, live in bliss, was he at peace, was not he, too, merely a seeker, a man athirst? Was it not necessary for him, a long-parched man, to drink again and again at sacred springs, at the sacrifice, at the books, at the dialogues of the Brahmans? Why was it necessary for him, the faultless one, to wash away his sins every day, to strive for purification every day, all over again every day? Was *Atman* not in him, then? Did the wellspring not flow, then, in his own heart? It had to be found, the wellspring in one's own self, it had to be securely possessed! All else was a mere quest, a detour, an aberration.

Thus ran Siddhartha's thoughts, this was his thirst, this his sorrow.

Often he recited to himself the words from the *Chandogya Upanishad*: "Verily, the name of the *Brahman* is *satyam*—truly, he who knows this enters daily into the heavenly world." It often seemed near, that heavenly world, but he had never fully attained it, he had never quenched his ultimate thirst. And among all the wise and wisest men whom he knew, and whose instruction he enjoyed, there was none of them who had fully attained it, that heavenly world; who had fully quenched it, that eternal thirst.

"Govinda," Siddhartha said to his friend, "my dear Govinda, come with me under the banyan tree; we shall practice concentration."

They went to the banyan tree, they sat down, Siddhartha here, Govinda twenty paces further. As he was sitting down, ready to utter the *om*, Siddhartha repeated in a murmur the verse:

> "*Om* is the bow, the arrow is the soul,
> The *Brahman* is the arrow's goal,
> Which should be hit unswervingly."

When the customary period of the concentration practice had passed, Govinda arose. Evening had come; it was time to perform the ablution of the evening hour. He called Siddhartha's name. Siddhartha made no reply. Siddhartha sat in concentration; his eyes were fixed on a very distant goal; the tip of his tongue protruded slightly between his teeth; he seemed not to be breathing. Thus he sat, shrouded in concentration, thinking of *om*, his soul having been shot like an arrow at the *Brahman.*

Once, samanas had passed through Siddhartha's town, itinerant ascetics, three dried-up, burnt-out men, neither old nor young, with dusty and bloody shoulders, nearly nude, scorched by the sun, surrounded by solitude, strangers and enemies to the world, outsiders and emaciated jackals in the realm of human beings. Behind them wafted a hot smell of silent passion, of destructive duty, of pitiless liberation from the self.

In the evening, after the hour of contemplation, Siddhartha said to Govinda: "Tomorrow morning, my friend, Siddhartha will go to the samanas. He will become a samana."

Govinda turned pale when he heard those words and read the resolve in his friend's motionless features, a resolve as impossible to deflect as an arrow loosed from a bow. Immediately, at the first glance, Govinda realized: now it is beginning, now Siddhartha is going his way, now his destiny is beginning to germinate, and mine along with his. And he became as pale as a dry plantain peel.

"O Siddhartha," he called, "will your father allow you to?"

Siddhartha glanced over at him like a man awakening. With the speed of an arrow he read in Govinda's soul, he read the anguish there, he read the devotion.

"O Govinda," he said softly, "let us not waste words. Tomorrow at daybreak I shall begin the life of the samanas. Speak no more of it."

Siddhartha stepped into the room where his father was sitting on a palm-fiber mat, and stepped behind his father, and remained standing there until his father felt someone standing behind him. The Brahman said: "Is it you, Siddhartha? If so, say what you have come to say."

Siddhartha said: "With your permission, Father. I have come to tell you that I desire to leave your house tomorrow and to go to the ascetics. To become a samana is my desire. I hope my father will not oppose this."

The Brahman was silent, and for so long that in the small window the stars progressed and altered their configuration before the silence in the room came to an end. Mute and motionless stood the son, with arms crossed; mute and motionless sat the father on his mat, and the stars moved across the sky. Then the father said: "It is unseemly for a Brahman to speak violent and angry words. But indignation stirs my heart. I should not like to hear that request from your lips a second time."

Slowly the Brahman rose; Siddhartha stood mute, with arms crossed.

"What are you waiting for?" asked the father.

Siddhartha said: "You know what for."

Indignantly the father left the room; indignantly he sought his bed and lay down.

An hour later, since no sleep visited his eyes, the Brahman got up, paced to and fro, stepped out of the house. He looked in through the small window of the room, where he saw Siddhartha standing, with arms crossed, on the same spot. His light-colored outer garment glimmered palely. Uneasy at heart, his father returned to his bed.

An hour later, since no sleep visited his eyes, the Brahman got up again, paced to and fro, stepped in front of the house, saw that the moon had risen. He looked in through the window of the room, where Siddhartha was standing on the same spot, with arms crossed, the moonlight reflected on his bare shins. Anxious at heart, his father sought his bed.

And he came again an hour later, and came again two hours later, looked in through the small window, saw Siddhartha standing in the moonlight, in the starshine, in the darkness. And he came again from hour to hour, in silence, looked into the room, saw his son standing motionless, filled his heart with anger, filled his heart with unrest, filled his heart with fearfulness, filled it with sorrow.

And in the last hour of the night, before the day began, he returned, stepped into the room, saw the young man standing there, looking tall and seemingly a stranger.

"Siddhartha," he said, "what are you waiting for?"

"You know what for."

"Will you keep on standing and waiting like this until it is day, noon, evening?"

"I shall stand and wait."

"You will grow weary, Siddhartha."

"I shall grow weary."

"You will fall asleep, Siddhartha."

"I shall not fall asleep."

"You will die, Siddhartha."

"I shall die."

"And you would rather die than obey your father?"

"Siddhartha has always obeyed his father."

"And so you will give up your plan?"

"Siddhartha will do what his father tells him to."

The first light of day entered the room. The Brahman saw that Siddhartha's knees were trembling slightly. In Siddhartha's face he saw no trembling; his eyes were looking into the distance. Then his father realized that by now Siddhartha was no longer with him and at home, that he had already left him.

Siddhartha's father touched his shoulder.

He said: "You will go to the forest and be a samana. If you find salvation in the forest, come and teach me salvation. If you find disappointment, then come back and let us once more sacrifice to the gods together. Now go and kiss your mother; tell her where you are going. But, for me, it is time to go to the river and perform the first ablution."

He lifted his hand from his son's shoulder and went out. Siddhartha swayed to one side when he tried to walk. He brought his limbs under control, bowed to his father, and went to his mother to do as his father had said.

When, at the first daylight, he was slowly leaving the still-silent town on his stiff legs, near the last cottage there arose a shadow that had been crouching there; it joined the wanderer—it was Govinda.

"You have come," said Siddhartha, and smiled.

"I have come," said Govinda.

With the Samanas

On the evening of that day they overtook the ascetics, the dried-out ascetics, and offered to accompany them and obey them. They were accepted.

Siddhartha gave away his robe to a poor Brahman on the road. All he still wore was a loincloth and an untailored, earth-colored wrap. He ate only once a day, and the food was never cooked. He fasted for fifteen days. He fasted for twenty-eight days. The flesh wasted away from his thighs and cheeks. Dreams flickered hotly from his widened eyes, on his shriveling fingers the nails grew long, as did the dry, stubbly beard on his chin. His gaze became icy when he met women; his mouth twitched in contempt when he passed through a town with well-dressed people. He saw merchants doing business, princes leaving for the hunt, mourners lamenting their dead, whores offering their services, doctors busy with patients, priests determining the proper day to begin sowing, lovers in love, mothers nursing their children—and none of it was worth the trouble of a glance, it was all a lie, it all stank, it all stank of lies, it all gave the illusion of meaning and happiness and beauty, and it was all unacknowledged decay. The world had a bitter taste. Life was torment.

One goal was Siddhartha's and only one: to become empty, empty of thirst, empty of wishes, empty of dreams, empty of joy and sorrow. To die away from himself, no longer to be "I," to find repose with an emptied heart, to be ready for a miracle with thought liberated from ego: that was his goal. When all ego was overcome and dead, when every yearning and every impulse in the heart was silent, then the Ultimate had to awaken, that innermost part of his being which is no longer the self—the great mystery.

Silently Siddhartha stood beneath the fierce vertical rays of the sun, burning with pain, burning with thirst, and he stood there until he no longer felt either pain or thirst. Silently he stood in the rainy season, the water dripping from his hair onto his chilled shoulders, onto his chilled hips and legs; and the penitent stood there until shoulders and legs no longer felt cold, until they were silent, until they were still. Silently he crouched in the brambles, blood oozing from his prickling skin, and pus from his abscesses; and Siddhartha remained there rigidly, remained there motionlessly, until no more blood flowed, until there was no more pricking, until there was no more burning.

Siddhartha sat up straight and learned to conserve his breath, learned how to make do with just a little breath, learned how to cut off his breath. He learned how to slacken his heartbeat, beginning with the breath; he learned how to diminish the number of his heartbeats until there were only a few, and practically none.

Instructed by the samana elder, Siddhartha practiced denial of self; he practiced concentration in accordance with new samana rules. A heron flew over the bamboo forest—and Siddhartha absorbed the heron into his soul; he flew over forest and mountain, he was the heron, he ate fish, he hungered with a heron's hunger, he spoke with a heron's croaking, he died a heron's death. A dead jackal lay on the sandy riverbank, and Siddhartha's soul slipped into the carcass; he was a dead jackal, he lay on the sand, he swelled up, stank, rotted, was torn apart by hyenas, was skinned by vultures, became a skeleton, turned to dust, blew away into the fields. And Siddhartha's soul returned; it had died, it had rotted, it had fallen into dust, it had tasted the dismal intoxication of the cycle of existences; filled with fresh thirst, like a hunter it was awaiting the gap through which it might escape the cycle, where causation would come to an end, where sorrowless eternity began. He mortified his senses, he mortified his power to remember, he stole out of his ego and into a thousand unfamiliar forms of creation; he was an animal, he was a carcass, he was stone, he was wood, he was water; and each time, upon awakening, he found himself again; the sun or the moon was shining; he was himself once again, he was moving through the cycle; he felt thirst, overcame his thirst, felt fresh thirst.

Many things did Siddhartha learn from the samanas; he learned how to take many paths away from self. He took the path of liberation from self through pain, through voluntary suffering and conquest of the pain, of hunger, thirst, fatigue. He took the path of liberation from self through meditation, by consciously emptying his mind of all ideas. He learned to take these and other paths; a thousand times he left his self behind, for hours and days at a time he remained in a state of nonself. But even though the paths led away from self, at the end they always led back to self. Even though Siddhartha escaped from self a thousand times, sojourning in the void, sojourning as an animal, as a stone, the return was unavoidable, inescapable the hour in which he found himself again, in sunlight or in moonlight, in shadow or in rain, and was once again "I" and Siddhartha, and once again felt the torment of the cycle that was imposed on him.

Alongside him lived Govinda, his shadow, taking the same paths, subjecting himself to the same efforts. Seldom did they say to each other any more than their duty and exercises required. At times they walked through the villages together to beg for food for themselves and their teachers.

"What do you think, Govinda?" Siddhartha said on one of these mendicant rounds, "What do you think? Have we made any progress? Have we reached any goals?"

Govinda answered: "We have learned, and we are continuing to learn. You will be a great samana, Siddhartha. You have learned every exercise quickly, the old samanas have admired you often. Some day you will be a saint, O Siddhartha."

Siddhartha said: "It just does not seem so to me, my friend. What I have learned from the samanas up to this day, O Govinda, I could have learned more quickly and more simply. I could have learned it in any tavern in a prostitutes' district, my friend, among the teamsters and the dice players."

Govinda said: "Siddhartha is joking with me. How could you have learned concentration, retention of breath, insensibility to hunger and pain, there among those miserable creatures?"

And Siddhartha said softly, as if speaking to himself: "What is concentration? What is the ability to leave one's body? What is fasting? What is retention of breath? It is a flight from the self, it is a brief escape from the torment of being 'I,' it is a brief numbing of the mind to counter pain and the senselessness of life. The same escape, the same brief numbing is found by the ox drover in his inn when he drinks a few bowls of rice wine or fermented coconut milk. Then he no longer feels his self, then he no longer feels the pains of life, then he finds a brief numbing of the mind. When he has dozed off over his bowl of rice wine, he finds the same thing that Siddhartha and Govinda find when, in lengthy exercises, they are released from their bodies and dwell in the nonself. It is thus, O Govinda."

Govinda said: "You speak thus, O friend, and yet you know that Siddhartha is not a drover, and a samana is not a drunkard. Yes, the drinker is numbed for a while; yes, he finds a brief escape and rest, but he comes out of his delusion and finds that everything is still the same; he has not grown wiser, he has not gathered knowledge, he has not risen a few steps higher."

And Siddhartha said with a smile: "I do not know, I have never been a drinker. But that I, Siddhartha, find only a brief numbing in my exercises and bouts of concentration, and that I am just as far removed from wisdom and salvation as a child in the womb: this I know, O Govinda, this I know."

And on another occasion, when Siddhartha left the forest with Govinda to beg some food in the village for their brothers and teachers, Siddhartha began to speak, saying: "Well, now, O Govinda, are we on the right path? Are we perhaps approaching knowledge? Are we perhaps approaching salvation? Or are we not rather going around in a circle—we, who after all thought we could escape the cycle of existences?"

Govinda said: "We have learned much, Siddhartha; much still remains to be learned. We are not going around in a circle, we are proceeding upward; the circle is a spiral, and we have already climbed many a step."

Siddhartha answered: "How old do you think our samana elder is, our venerable teacher?"

Govinda said: "Our elder is about sixty years old."

And Siddhartha: "He has become sixty years old and has never attained *nirvana*. He will become seventy and eighty, and you and I shall become just as old, and shall do exercises, and shall fast, and shall meditate. But we shall never attain *nirvana*, not he, not we. O Govinda, I believe that, of all the samanas who exist, perhaps not one, not one, will attain *nirvana*. We find consolations, we find ways to numb the mind, we learn technical skills for deceiving ourselves. But the essential, the path of paths, that we do not find."

Govinda said: "Please do not pronounce such terrifying words, Siddhartha! How could it be that, among so many learned men, among so many Brahmans, among so many severe and venerable samanas, among so many questing men, so many assiduous men, so many holy men, no one will find the path of paths?"

But Siddhartha said, in a voice containing as much sadness as mockery, in a soft, slightly sad, slightly mocking voice: "Soon, Govinda, your friend will abandon this path of the samanas, which he has followed with you for so long. I am suffering from thirst, O Govinda, and on this long samana path my thirst has not diminished one whit. I have always thirsted for knowledge, I have always been full of questions. I have questioned the Brahmans, year after year, and I have questioned the sacred Vedas, year after year. Perhaps, O Govinda, it would have been just as good, it would have been just as clever and just as beneficial if I had questioned the hornbill or the chimpanzee.[5] I have needed a long time, and that time is not yet up, to learn this, O Govinda: that no one can learn a thing! I believe firmly that in reality the thing we call 'learning' does not exist. O my friend, all there is is a knowledge, which is everywhere, which is Atman, which is in me and in you and in every being. And so I am beginning to believe that this knowledge has no worse enemy than the desire to know, than learning."

At that point Govinda stopped short on their path, raised his hands, and said: "Siddhartha, please do not alarm your friend with such talk! Truly, your words awaken anxiety in my heart. And just think: where would the sacredness of prayers be, where would the venerableness of the Brahman class be, or the holiness of the samanas, if things were as you say, if there were no such thing as learning?! What, O Siddhartha, what would then become of everything on earth that is holy, valuable, and venerable?!"

And Govinda murmured a verse to himself, a verse from an Upanishad:

"He who in contemplation, with purified mind, immerses himself in Atman,
  Inexpressible in words is his heart's bliss."

But Siddhartha was silent. He was thinking about the words Govinda had spoken to him, and thought the words through to their very end.

"Yes," he thought, standing there with lowered head, "what would still be left of everything that seemed holy to us? What is left? What stands up to the test?" And he shook his head.

On one occasion, when the two young men had lived about three years with the samanas, participating in their exercises, there came to them by many direct and indirect routes a notice, a rumor, a legend: that a man had appeared, Gotama by name, the Sublime One, the Buddha, who had overcome the sorrow of the world within himself, bringing the wheel of rebirths to a halt. He was said to be traveling through the land, surrounded by disciples, without possessions, without a home, without a wife, in the yellow mantle of an ascetic, but with a serene brow, a beatified man before whom Brahmans and princes were bowing, becoming his pupils.

This legend, this rumor, this tale, made itself heard, rose upward like a fragrance, here and there. In the towns the Brahmans were talking

---

[5] An outright error on Hesse's part. Chimpanzees are found only in Africa.

about it; in the forest, the samanas. Again and again the name of Gotama, the Buddha, reached the young men's ears, for good and for bad, in praise and in revilement.

Just as when the plague reigns in a land and the news arises that, in this place or that, there is a man, a sage, a knowledgeable one, whose mere words or insufflation are able to cure every victim of the epidemic; just as that news then spreads through the land, and everyone talks about it, many believing, many doubting, but many immediately setting out to seek the sage, the helper: so did that legend spread through the land, that fragrant legend of Gotama, the Buddha, the sage from the clan of the Sakyas. The believers said that he possessed the loftiest knowledge, that he remembered his previous lives, that he had attained *nirvana* and would never return to the cycle of existences, would never again sink into the troubled current of created forms. Many splendid and unbelievable things were reported of him; he had performed miracles, he had conquered the Devil, he had conversed with the gods. But his enemies and the unbelievers said that this Gotama was a vain seducer, that he spent his days in luxury, looked down on sacrifices, lacked scholarly attainments, and was unfamiliar with either ascetic exercises or castigation.

Sweet-sounding was the legend of Buddha; a magical fragrance emanated from these reports. The world was indeed ill, life was hard to bear—and, behold, here a spring seemed to be welling up, here a messenger's call seemed to be sounding, consoling, mild, full of noble promises. Wherever the rumor about the Buddha was heard, throughout the Indian realms, the young men hearkened, felt a longing, felt a hope; and among the Brahman's sons of the towns and villages every wanderer and stranger was welcome if he brought word of him, the Sublime One, the Sakyamuni.

To the samanas in the forest as well, to Siddhartha as well, to Govinda as well, the legend had made its way, slowly, drop by drop, each drop laden with hope, each drop laden with doubt. They spoke of it little, for the samana elder was no friend of this legend. He had heard that that alleged Buddha had formerly been an ascetic and had lived in the forest, but had then returned to luxuries and secular pleasures; and he had a low opinion of this Gotama.

"O Siddhartha," Govinda said to his friend on one occasion, "today I was in the village, and a Brahman invited me to come into his house; in his house there was a Brahman's son from Magadha, who has seen the Buddha with his own eyes and has heard him preaching. Truly, the breath in my chest ached me then, and I thought to myself: 'If only I too, if only both of us, Siddhartha and I, might live to see that hour in which we hear the doctrine from the very lips of that Perfect One.' Tell me, friend, shall we not go there, too, and listen to the doctrine from the Buddha's lips?"

Siddhartha said: "O Govinda, I had always thought that Govinda would stay with the samanas; I had always thought his goal was to become sixty and seventy years old, continuing all the while to practice the arts and exercises that adorn a samana. But see, I had known too little of Govinda, I had known too little about his heart. So, best of friends, you now wish to make a journey and go where the Buddha is proclaiming his doctrine!"

Govinda said: "You are pleased to mock me. May you go on mocking all the same, Siddhartha! But has no desire, no inclination, awakened in you, as well, to hear this teaching? And did you not once tell me you would not follow the path of the samanas much longer?"

Then Siddhartha laughed after his manner, the tone of his voice taking on a shade of sadness and a shade of mockery, and he said: "Well, Govinda, you have spoken well, your recollection was correct. But please also recollect that other thing you heard me say, that I have become distrustful and weary of teaching and learning, and that I have little faith in words that come to us from teachers. But, all right, my dear friend, I am prepared to hear that doctrine—although I believe in my heart that we have already tasted the finest fruits of that doctrine."

Govinda said: "Your preparedness pleases my heart. But tell me, how could that be possible? How could Gotama's doctrine, which we have not yet heard, already have disclosed its finest fruits to us?"

Siddhartha said: "Let us enjoy those fruits and wait for the rest, O Govinda! But these fruits, for which we are already obliged to Gotama, consist in his calling us away from the samanas! Whether he has other and better things to give us, O friend, let us wait and see with a calm heart."

On that same day Siddhartha informed the samana elder of his decision to leave him. He informed the elder of this with the courtesy and modesty befitting a younger man and a pupil. But the samana flew into a rage because the two young men wished to leave him; he raised his voice and indulged in coarse insults.

Govinda was frightened and became embarrassed, but Siddhartha inclined his lips to Govinda's ear and whispered to him: "Now I am going to show the old man that I have learned something from him."

Placing himself right in front of the samana, with concentrated psychic powers, he caught the old man's gaze with his own, spellbound him, reduced him to silence, robbed him of his will, subjected him to his own will, and commanded him to perform in silence whatever he desired him to. The old man became mute, his eyes grew rigid, his will was paralyzed, his arms hung down limply; powerless, he had succumbed to Siddhartha's enchantment. But Siddhartha's thoughts took control of the samana, who had to carry out their orders. And so the old man bowed several times, executed gestures of blessing, and stammered out a pious wish for a good journey. And the young men returned his bows, giving thanks, returned his good wishes, and left, saying farewell.

On the way Govinda said: "O Siddhartha, you learned more from the samanas than I knew. It is difficult, it is very difficult, to cast a spell on an old samana. Truly, had you remained there, you would soon have learned how to walk on water."

"I do not desire to walk on water," said Siddhartha. "Let old samanas content themselves with arts of that kind."

Gotama

In the town of Savatthi[6] every child knew the name of Buddha the Sublime One, and every household was prepared to fill the alms bowl of Gotama's disciples, who begged in silence. Just outside the town lay the place where Gotama most liked to stay, the Jetavana grove, which the wealthy merchant Anathapindika, a devoted worshipper of the Sublime One, had presented as a gift to him and his followers.

It was this neighborhood that had been indicated in the stories and replies that were communicated to the two young ascetics during their quest for the place where Gotama abode. And when they arrived in Savatthi, at the very first house before whose door they remained standing in supplication, they were offered food; they accepted the food, and Siddhartha asked the woman who handed them the food:

"Gladly, you charitable woman, gladly would we learn where the Buddha abides, the Most Venerable One, for we are two samanas from the forest, and we have come to see him, the Perfect One, and hear the doctrine from his own lips."

The woman said: "Truly, you have stopped at the right place, you samanas from the forest. Let me tell you that the Sublime One abides in Jetavana, in Anathapindika's garden. There, wanderers, you can spend the night, for there is enough room there for the countless people who come flocking to hear the doctrine from his lips."

Thereupon Govinda rejoiced and, full of joy, he called: "Well, then, so our goal is attained and our journey at an end! But tell us, mother

---

[6] The form "Savathi" in the German text is incorrect either in Pali or in Sanskrit. See the Glossary under "Savatthi."

of wanderers, do you know him, the Buddha, have you seen him with your own eyes?"

The woman said: "Many times have I seen him, the Sublime One. Many days I have seen him walking through the lanes, silently, in his yellow robe, silently holding out his alms bowl at the house doors, and bearing away the filled bowl."

Govinda listened in delight, and wanted to ask and hear much more. But Siddhartha urged him to continue the journey. They gave thanks, left, and hardly needed to ask the way, because a large number of pilgrims and monks from Gotama's community were on their way to Jetavana. And when they reached it at night, there were constant new arrivals, calling out and speaking as they sought and received lodging. The two samanas, accustomed to life in the forest, found shelter quickly and noiselessly, and rested there till morning.

At sunrise they saw in amazement how great a throng of believers and the idly curious had spent the night there. On every path in the splendid grove yellow-robed monks were walking, they were sitting here and there under the trees, immersed in contemplation or in spiritual conversation; the shady gardens looked like a town full of people swarming like bees. Most of the monks set out with their alms bowls to gather food in town for the midday meal, the only one of the day. Even the Buddha himself, the Enlightened One, used to make his mendicant rounds in the morning.

Siddhartha saw him, and recognized him at once, as if a god had pointed him out to him. He saw him, a simple man in a yellow monk's robe, carrying his alms bowl in his hand as he walked calmly onward.

"Look!" said Siddhartha softly to Govinda. "This man is the Buddha."

Govinda looked attentively at the monk in the yellow robe, who seemed to differ in no way from the hundreds of other monks. And soon Govinda, too, realized: this is the one. And they followed him and observed him.

The Buddha went his way modestly and lost in thought; his calm face was neither merry nor sad, but seemed to be gently smiling inwardly. With a concealed smile, calmly, peacefully, not unlike a healthy child, the Buddha walked, wore his robe, and planted his feet just like all his monks, in accordance with precise rules. But his face and his step, his calmly lowered gaze, his hands held calmly at his side, and indeed every finger of his calmly held hands, spoke of peace, spoke of perfection, sought nothing, imitated nothing, but breathed softly in unfading repose, in unfading light, in unassailable peace.

Thus Gotama walked toward the town to gather alms, and the two samanas recognized him solely by the perfection of his repose, by the calmness of his figure, in which there was no trace of seeking, desiring, imitating, or striving, only light and peace.

"Today we shall hear the doctrine from his own lips," said Govinda.

Siddhartha made no reply. He was not so curious about the doctrine; he did not believe that it would teach him anything new; after all, both he and Govinda had heard the contents of this Buddhist doctrine time and again, although only from second- and third-hand reports. But he looked attentively at Gotama's head, at his shoulders, at his feet, at his hands held calmly at his side; and it seemed to him as if every joint of every finger of those hands were doctrine, speaking and breathing truth, wafting it abroad like a fragrance, emitting it like light. This man, this Buddha, was filled with truth down to the least movement of his smallest finger. This man was holy. Never had Siddhartha revered any person, never had he loved any person, as he did this man.

The two followed the Buddha all the way to town and returned in silence, for they themselves intended to refrain from eating that day. They saw Gotama returning, they saw him eat his meal in the circle of his disciples—what he ate would not have filled a bird—and they saw him withdraw into the shade of the mango trees.

But in the evening, when the heat abated and all those in the camp became lively and gathered together, they heard the Buddha preach. They heard his voice, and it, too, was perfect, it was perfectly calm, it was full of peace. Gotama preached the doctrine of suffering, the origin of suffering, and the way to abolish suffering. Tranquilly and clearly his calm words flowed. Life meant suffering, the world was full of sorrow, but deliverance from sorrow had been found: he who followed the Buddha's path found deliverance.

In a gentle but firm voice the Sublime One spoke; he taught the Four Basic Truths, he taught the Eightfold Way; patiently he followed the customary path of the doctrine, with its parables, with its repetitions; brightly and calmly his voice hovered over the listeners, like a light, like a starry sky.

When the Buddha—night had already fallen—ended his speech, many pilgrims stepped forward and requested admittance to the community, taking refuge in the Law. And Gotama admitted them, saying: "You have heard the teaching well, it is well proclaimed. So then, step up and walk in holiness, to prepare an end to all sorrow."

Behold, thereupon Govinda, too, the shy one, stepped forth, saying: "I, too, take refuge in the Sublime One and his Law," and requested admittance to the band of disciples, and was admitted.

Immediately afterward, when the Buddha had retired to his night's rest, Govinda turned to Siddhartha, saying earnestly: "Siddhartha, it is not for me to reproach you. We have both listened to the Sublime One, we have both heard the doctrine. Govinda has listened to the doctrine, he has taken refuge in it. But you, whom I honor, will you not also walk the road to salvation? Will you hesitate, will you still wait?"

Siddhartha awoke, as if from slumber, when he heard Govinda's words. For a long while he gazed at Govinda's face. Then he said softly, in a voice free from mockery: "Govinda, my friend, now you have taken the step, now you have chosen the path. O Govinda, you have always been my friend, you have always walked one step behind me. I have often thought: 'Will not Govinda ever take a step on his own, without me, from his own soul?' Behold, now you have become a man and are choosing your path yourself. May you follow it to the end, O my friend! May you find salvation!"

Govinda, who did not yet completely understand, repeated his question in an impatient tone: "But speak, I beg of you, my dear friend! Tell me—and it surely cannot be otherwise—that you, too, my learned friend, will take refuge in the sublime Buddha!"

Siddhartha laid his hand on Govinda's shoulder: "You have failed to hear my words of benediction, O Govinda. I repeat them: May you follow this path to the end! May you find salvation!"

At that moment Govinda realized that his friend had taken leave of him, and he began to weep.

"Siddhartha!" he called lamentingly.

Siddhartha spoke to him like a friend: "Do not forget, Govinda, that you now belong to the samanas of the Buddha! You have renounced home and parents, renounced ancestry and possessions, renounced your own will, renounced friendship. That is what the doctrine desires, that is what the Sublime One desires. You yourself have desired it. Tomorrow, O Govinda, I shall leave you."

For a long while still, the friends walked through the grove, for a long while they lay down but could not fall asleep. And ever anew Govinda urged his friend to tell him why he did not wish to take refuge in Gotama's doctrine, what flaw he could possibly find in that doctrine. But each time Siddhartha refused, saying: "Be contented, Govinda! The Sublime One's doctrine is very good; how should I find a flaw in it?"

Very early in the morning a follower of the Buddha, one of his oldest monks, walked through the garden, calling after all those who had taken refuge in the Law as novices, so he could dress them in the yellow robe and instruct them in the rudimentary teachings and duties of their order. Thereupon Govinda tore himself away, embraced the friend of his youth once more, and joined the group of novices.

But Siddhartha walked through the grove deep in thought.

Then Gotama, the Sublime One, came across him; and when he greeted him respectfully, and the Buddha's eyes were so full of kindness and calm, the young man took heart and asked the Venerable One for permission to speak to him. Silently the Sublime One nodded his consent.

Siddhartha said: "Yesterday, O Sublime One, I was privileged to hear your marvelous teachings. Together with my friend I came here from far off to hear the teachings. And now my friend will remain with your followers; he has taken refuge in you. But I am continuing my wanderings again."

"As you please," said the Venerable One courteously.

"My words are much too bold," Siddhartha went on, "but I would not like to depart from the Sublime One without having told him honestly what I think. Will the Venerable One grant me another moment's audience?"

Silently the Buddha nodded his consent.

Siddhartha said: "One thing above all, O Most Venerable One, I have admired in your teachings. Everything in your teachings is perfectly clear and fully proven; you show the world to be a perfect chain, never and nowhere interrupted, an eternal chain fashioned out of causes and effects. Never before has this been seen so clearly, never so irrefutably presented; truly, every Brahman's heart must beat more jubilantly in his breast when, through your teachings, he sees the world as being perfectly interconnected, without a gap, clear as a crystal, not dependent on chance, not dependent on gods. Whether it is good or evil, whether life in it is sorrow or joy, is not the immediate question— perhaps it is a question of no importance. But the unity of the world, the connectedness of all events, the fact that all things, great and small, are bounded by the same current, by the same law of causality, becoming, and dying—that shines brightly forth from your sublime teachings, O Perfect One. And yet, according to your own doctrine, this unity and consequentiality of all things is interrupted in one place; through a small gap there flows into this unified world something strange to it, something new, something that did not previously exist, and that cannot be shown or proven: it is your doctrine of overcoming the world, of salvation. But by this small gap, by this small breach, the whole eternal and unified world law is once again shattered and canceled. Please forgive me for pointing out this objection."

Gotama had listened to him calmly, unruffled. In his kindly, courteous, and clear voice he now said, the Perfect One: "You have heard the doctrine, O Brahman's son, and you are fortunate in having meditated on it so profoundly. You have found a gap in it, a flaw. I hope you will continue to meditate on it. But let me warn you, you thirster after knowledge, against the jungle of opinions and quarreling over mere words. Opinions are completely unimportant, whether they are beautiful or ugly, clever or foolish; anyone can adhere to them or reject them. But the doctrine you have heard from me is not an opinion of mine; its goal is not to explain the world to thirsters after knowledge. Its goal is different; its goal is deliverance from suffering. This is what Gotama preaches, and nothing else."

"Please, O Sublime One, do not be cross with me," the young man said. "I did not speak to you that way in order to pick a quarrel with you, a quarrel over words. Truly, you are right, opinions are quite unimportant. But let me say just one thing more: Not for a moment have I had doubts about you. I have not doubted for a moment that you are the Buddha, that you have attained the goal, that highest goal which so many thousands of Brahmans and Brahmans' sons are seeking. You have found deliverance from death. It has become yours through your own quest, on your own path, by means of thought, concentration, realization, enlightenment. It did not become yours through teachings! And—this is my thought, O Sublime One—no one will achieve salvation through teachings! O Venerable One, you will not be able to inform and tell a single person in words and by means of teachings what happened to you in the hour of your enlightenment! The doctrine of the enlightened Buddha contains a great deal, it teaches many to live righteously, to shun evil. But one thing this doctrine, so clear, so venerable, does not contain: it does not contain the secret of what the Sublime One himself experienced, he alone among the hundreds of thousands. This is what I thought and realized when I heard the doctrine. This is why I am continuing my wanderings—not to seek another, better doctrine, because I know there is none, but to leave behind all teachings and all teachers, and either to attain my goal alone or to die. But I shall often remember this day, O Sublime One, and this hour, in which my eyes beheld a saint."

The Buddha's eyes were calmly fixed on the ground; his inscrutable face beamed calmly in perfect equanimity.

The Venerable One said slowly: "May your thoughts not be errors! May you reach your goal! But tell me: have you seen the throng of my samanas, of my many brothers who have taken refuge in the Law? And do you believe, samana stranger, that it would be better for all of them to abandon the Law and return to the life of the world and its pleasures?"

"Far from me is such a thought!" Siddhartha cried. "May they all remain in the Law, may they attain their goal! It is not for me to stand in judgment over another man's life! Solely for myself, for me alone, I must judge, I must choose, I must reject. O Sublime One, we samanas seek deliverance from the self. Now, if I were one of your disciples, O Venerable One, I fear it might occur that my self would find repose and be delivered only seemingly, only deceptively, but that it would actually live on and develop further—because I would then have turned the Law, my adherence to it, my love for you, and the monastic community, into my new self!"

With a half-smile, with unshakable brightness and friendliness, Gotama looked the stranger in the eye and sent him on his way with a barely visible gesture.

"You are clever, O samana," said the Venerable One. "You can speak cleverly, my friend. Beware of too much cleverness!"

The Buddha walked away, and his gaze and half-smile remained engraved in Siddhartha's memory forever.

"I have never seen anyone gaze and smile, sit and walk, that way," he thought; "truly I wish I could also gaze and smile, sit and walk, that way, with such freedom, such venerableness, such concealment, such openness, such childlikeness, and such mystery. Truly, such a gaze and stride belong only to a person who has penetrated into his innermost self. Well, I, too, will strive to penetrate into my innermost self."

"I have seen a person," Siddhartha's thoughts continued, "a single person, in whose presence I had to cast down my eyes. Never again will I cast down my eyes in anyone's presence, not anyone's. From now on, no doctrine will entice me, since this person's doctrine has not enticed me."

"The Buddha has robbed me," Siddhartha's thoughts continued, "he has robbed me, but he has bestowed even more on me. He has robbed me of my friend, who used to believe in me and now believes in him, who used to be my shadow and is now Gotama's shadow. But he has bestowed on me Siddhartha, myself."

Awakening

When Siddhartha left the grove in which the Buddha, the Perfect One, remained behind, in which Govinda remained behind, he felt that in that grove his previous life, too, had remained behind him and had separated itself from him. As he walked on slowly, he pondered over that feeling, which filled his mind completely. He thought it over profoundly; as if sinking into deep waters, he let himself reach the bottom of that feeling, all the way to where the causes reside; for it seemed to him that to recognize causes is precisely what thinking means, and that only thereby do feelings become firm realizations, which are no longer lost, but become substantial and begin to diffuse their contents.

As he walked on slowly, Siddhartha pondered. He ascertained that he was no longer a youth, but had become a man. He ascertained that something had left him behind, just as a snake is left behind by its old skin, that there was no longer present within him something that had accompanied him throughout his youth and had belonged to him: the wish to have teachers and to hear teachings. The last teacher who had appeared on his path—even him, the loftiest and wisest teacher, the holiest, the Buddha—he had left behind; he had had to part from him, he had been unable to accept his doctrine.

Deep in thought, he walked on more slowly, asking himself: "But what is it, then, that you wanted to learn from teachings and from teachers, but which they—who taught you a lot—were nevertheless unable to teach you?" And he discovered: "It was the self whose meaning and nature I wanted to learn. It was the self that I wanted to be free of, that I wanted to overcome. But I could not overcome it, I could only deceive it, I could only run away from it, I could only hide from it. Truly, nothing in the world has occupied my thoughts as much as this self of mine, this riddle of my living, of my being one person sundered and separated from all the rest, of my being Siddhartha! And there is nothing in the world I know less about than myself, Siddhartha!"

He who had been pondering as he slowly walked on now came to a halt, in the clutch of this thought; and at once there emanated from this thought yet another one, a new thought, formulated thus: "That I know nothing of myself, that Siddhartha has remained so strange and unfamiliar to me, has one cause, just one: I was afraid of myself, I was running away from myself! I was seeking *Atman*, I was seeking *Brahman*, I was determined to dismember my self and tear away its layers of husk in order to find in its unknown innermost recess the kernel at the heart of all those layers, the *Atman*, life, the divine principle, the Ultimate. But in so doing I was losing myself."

Siddhartha opened his eyes and looked around him; a smile spread over his face, and a profound sensation of awakening from lengthy dreams flowed through him down to his toes. And at once he was on his way again, walking swiftly, like a man who knows what he must do.

"Oh," he thought, drawing a deep breath of relief, "now I shall not allow Siddhartha to slip away from me again. No longer shall I begin my thinking and my life with *Atman* and the sorrow of the world. No longer shall I mortify and dismember myself in order to find a mystery in back of the ruins. I shall no longer be instructed by the *Yoga Veda*, or the *Atharva Veda*, or the ascetics, or any other doctrine whatsoever. I shall learn from myself, be a pupil of myself; I shall get to know myself, the mystery of Siddhartha."

He looked around as if he were seeing the world for the first time.

The world was beautiful, the world was full of variety, the world was strange and puzzling! Here was blue, here was yellow, here was green; sky flowed, and river; forest jutted upward, and mountains; everything beautiful, everything puzzling and magical; and, in the midst of it all, he, Siddhartha, awakening, on the path to himself. All this, all this yellow and blue, river and forest, passed into Siddhartha through his eyes for the first time; it was no longer the sorcery of Mara, it was no longer the veil of *maya*, it was no longer the meaningless, accidental multiplicity of the world of phenomena, contemptible to the philosophical Brahman, who scorns multiplicity and seeks unity. Blue was blue, river was river; and if the One, the divine principle, lay concealed even in the blueness and river within Siddhartha, it was precisely the nature and meaning of that divine principle to be here yellow, here blue, there sky, there forest, and here Siddhartha. Meaning and essence were not somewhere or other in back of things, they were in them, in everything.

"How deaf and obtuse I have been!" he thought as he walked on swiftly. "When someone reads a piece of writing and wants to find out what it means, he does not feel contempt for the written signs and letters, calling them illusion, chance, and a valueless husk, but he reads them, he studies and loves them, letter by letter. But I, who wanted to read the book of the world and the book of my own nature, I have held the signs and letters in contempt, for the sake of a preassumed interpretation; I called the world of phenomena an illusion, I called my eyes and my tongue an accident, valueless phenomena. No, that is all over; I have awakened, I have really awakened and I have just been born today."

As Siddhartha was thinking that last thought, he came to a halt again, all of a sudden, as if a snake lay on the path before him.

For suddenly this, too, had become clear to him: since he was really like a man who had awakened or had just been born, he had to begin his life afresh, from the very outset. When, on that same morning, he had left the grove of Jetavana, the grove of that Sublime One, already awakening, already on the path to himself, it had been his intention, and had seemed a natural and obvious course to him, to return home to his father after his years of ascetic life. But now, only at the moment when he stopped short as if a snake lay on his path, did he awaken to this insight as well: "Now, I am no longer the man I was, I am no longer an ascetic, I am no longer a priest, I am no longer a Brahman. So, what am I to do at home with my father? Study? Perform sacrifices? Practice concentration? All that is past, all that no longer lies along my path."

Siddhartha stood there motionless, and for the space of a moment and a breath his heart grew chill; he felt it cold in his breast like a little animal, a bird or a hare, when he saw how alone he was. For years he had been homeless and had not felt it. Now he felt it. Up to now, even when lost most fully in ritual concentration,[7] he had been his father's son, he had been a Brahman, a man of high rank, an intellectual. Now he was only Siddhartha, the man who had awakened, and nothing more. He drew a deep breath, and for a moment he was cold and shuddered. No one was so alone as he. There was no nobleman who did not belong to the nobility; no artisan who did not belong among the artisans and could not take refuge with them, sharing their way of life, speaking their language. There was no Brahman who was not numbered among the Brahmans, living with them; no ascetic who did not find refuge in his status as a samana. And even the most forlorn hermit in the forest was not solitary and alone; he, too, was sheltered by a sense of belonging; he, too, belonged to a group that meant home to him. Govinda had become a monk, and a thousand monks were his brothers, wore the same garment, shared the same faith, spoke his language. But he, Siddhartha, where did he belong? Whose life would he share? Whose language would he speak?

From that moment, in which the world melted away from him all around, in which he stood alone like a star in the sky—from that moment of chill and despondency—Siddhartha emerged, more himself than before, his powers more firmly compacted. He felt that this had been the final shudder of awakening, the final throe of birth. And at once he set out again, beginning to walk swiftly and impatiently, no longer homeward, no longer to his father, no longer looking back.

---

[7] Another possible translation (Hesse possibly had both interpretations in mind) is: "even when he had disappeared from sight in the remotest places."

PART TWO

Kamala

Siddhartha learned something new with every step of his journey, for the world was transformed and his heart was under an enchantment. He saw the sun rise above the wooded mountains and set above the distant palm-bordered beach. At night he saw the stars patterned in the sky, and the moon's sickle floating in the blue like a boat. He saw trees, stars, animals, clouds, rainbows, cliffs, plants, flowers, brook and river, the flashing of dew on the bushes in the morning, distant, tall mountains blue and pale; birds sang and bees buzzed, the wind blew silvery in the rice paddies. All this, multiple and diversified, had always been there, the sun and moon had always shone, rivers had always roared and bees had buzzed; but in earlier days all this had been nothing to Siddhartha but a transitory, deceptive veil before his eyes, looked upon with mistrust, only existing in order to be penetrated and annihilated by thought, since it was not essence, since essence lay beyond the visible, on its far side. But now his liberated eyes tarried on the near side; he saw and appreciated the visible, he sought a home in this world; he did not seek essence or aim for any "beyond." The world was beautiful when looked at in this way, without a quest for the transcendent; it was so simple, so childlike. The moon and stars were beautiful, the brook and its banks were beautiful, forest and crag, goat and rose beetle, flower and butterfly. It was beautiful and lovely to wander through the world this way, so like a child, so wide awake, so open to your surroundings, so free from mistrust. The sun burned down on your head in a different way, the forest shade cooled you in a different way, the brook and the cistern tasted different, and so did the gourd and the plantain. The days were short, the nights were short; every hour sped rapidly by like a sail on the sea, and beneath that sail a ship laden with treasures, laden with joys. Siddhartha saw a tribe of monkeys moving through the lofty forest ceiling, high up in the branches, and heard a wild chant of desire. Siddhartha saw a ram pursue a ewe and mate with her. In a reedy lake he saw a pike hunting as hunger came over it in the evening; before it whole schools of young fish leapt out of the water, fearful, wriggling, flashing; power and passion arose like a penetrating scent from the rushing eddies that the violent hunter created.

All this had always existed, but he had not seen it; he had not been present. Now he was present, he belonged to it all. Through his eyes light and shadow raced, through his heart stars and moon raced.

As he journeyed, Siddhartha also recalled all his experiences in the garden of Jetavana, the teachings he had heard there, the divine Buddha, his leavetaking from Govinda, his conversation with the Sublime One. He recalled once more his own words that he had spoken to the Sublime One, every word, and with amazement he realized that he had said things then that were actually beyond his ken at the time. What he had said to Gotama, that his (the Buddha's) treasure and secret were not his doctrine but the ineffable, unteachable experience he had once had in the hour of his enlightenment—it was this very thing that he was now setting out to experience, that he was now beginning to experience. He now had to experience himself. Of course, he had already long known that his self was *Atman*, of the same eternal essence as *Brahman*. But he had never really found that self, because he had tried to catch it with the net of thought. Even if the body was certainly not the self, and the play of the senses was not it, nevertheless, thought was not the self, either, nor was the intellect, nor acquired wisdom, nor the acquired art of drawing conclusions and spinning new thoughts out of preexisting ones. No, this world of thought was also terrestrial, and you arrived at no goal when you killed the accidental "I" of the senses but instead fattened the accidental "I" of thinking and scholarship. Thoughts and senses were both fine things behind which ultimate meaning lay concealed; both should be listened to, both should be played with, neither of them should be condemned or overrated, by means of both you should try to hear the secret voices of the innermost essence. He decided to strive solely for what the voice commanded him to strive for; to linger over nothing unless the voice advised him to. Why had Gotama once, in the hour of hours, sat down beneath the *bo* tree, where he received enlightenment? He had heard a voice, a voice in his own heart, ordering him to seek repose beneath that tree, and he had preferred neither castigation nor sacrifices, neither bath nor prayer, neither eating nor drinking, neither sleep nor dream, but had obeyed that voice. To obey in that fashion, not a command from outside but only that voice, to be thus prepared, was good, was necessary; nothing else was necessary.

During the night, while sleeping in the straw hut of a ferryman by the river, Siddhartha had a dream: Govinda stood before him, in a yellow ascetic's robe. Govinda looked sad, sadly he asked: "Why have you deserted me?" Then he embraced Govinda, threw his arms around him, and as he drew him to his breast and kissed him, it was no longer Govinda, but a woman, and from the woman's robe a milk-laden breast was exposed; Siddhartha lay and drank from it; the milk from that breast tasted sweet and strong. It tasted of woman and man, of sun and forest, of animal and flower, of every fruit, of every pleasure. It made him drunk and unconscious.—When Siddhartha awoke, the pale river was glimmering through the door of the hut, and in the forest the dark cry of an owl resounded, deep and melodious.

When the day began, Siddhartha asked his host, the ferryman, to take him across the river. The ferryman took him across the river on his bamboo raft; the wide waters had a red glimmer in the morning light.

"This is a beautiful river," he said to his companion.

"Yes," said the ferryman, "a very beautiful river; I love it above all other things. I have often listened to it, I have often looked into its eyes, and I have always learned from it. You can learn a lot from a river."

"Thank you, my benefactor," said Siddhartha as he climbed onto the other bank. "I have no gift for you, my dear man, such as one gives to one's host, nor can I pay you. I am a homeless man, a Brahman's son and a samana."

"I could see that," said the ferryman, "and I did not expect any payment from you, nor a guest's gift. You will give me the gift another time."

"You think so?" said Siddhartha merrily.

"Absolutely. This, too, I have learned from the river: everything returns! You, too, samana, will return. Now farewell! Let your friendship be my pay. May you think of me when you sacrifice to the gods."

Both smiled as they parted. Siddhartha smiled as he rejoiced over the friendship and friendliness of the ferryman. "He is like Govinda," he thought with a smile; "everyone I meet on my journey is like Govinda. They are all grateful, even though they are the ones who deserve the thanks. They are all ready to serve me, they would all like to be my friends, to obey me without thinking hard about it. People are like children."

About midday he was walking through a village. In front of the clay huts children were tumbling about in the street, playing with gourd seeds and seashells, yelling and scuffling, but they all ran in fright from the strange samana. At the end of the village the path led across a brook, and at the edge of the brook a young woman was kneeling and washing clothes. When Siddhartha greeted her, she raised her head and looked up at him with a smile, so that he saw the gleam from the whites of her eyes. He called out a blessing on her, as is customary with travelers, and asked her how far it still was to the big town. Then she stood up and walked over to him; her moist lips were beautiful, glimmering in her young face. She exchanged jocular words with him, asked him if he had already eaten and if it was true that samanas slept alone at night in the forest and were not allowed to have any women with them. At the same time, she placed her left foot on his right and moved her body like a woman inviting a man to the style of lovemaking that the manuals call "climbing a tree."[8] Siddhartha felt his blood heat up and, since he recalled his dream at that moment, he stooped down slightly to the woman and, with his lips, kissed the brown tip of one breast. Looking up, he saw her face smiling, filled with desire, and her narrowed eyes beseeching him longingly.

Siddhartha, too, felt a longing, and felt the fountain of sex stirring; but, since he had never yet touched a woman, he hesitated for a moment, though his hands were already all set to reach out for her. And at that moment, with a shudder, he heard his inner voice, and the voice said no. Thereupon all the magic vanished from the young woman's smiling face; he no longer saw anything there but the moist eyes of a female animal in heat. In a friendly way he stroked her cheek, turned away from her, and with light steps disappeared from the disappointed woman's view into the bamboo grove.

Before evening of that day he reached a big town, and was happy, for he desired to be among people. For a long time he had lived in the forests, and the ferryman's straw hut, in which he had slept the night before, had been the first roof over his head in a long while.

Just outside town, near a beautiful grove enclosed by a hedge, the wanderer was met by a small train of male and female servants laden with baskets. In their midst, in a decorated sedan chair carried by four men, a woman, their mistress, sat on red cushions under a colorful canopy. Siddhartha remained standing at the entrance to the pleasure grove, watching the procession; he saw the servants, the maids, the baskets; he saw the sedan chair and saw the lady in the chair. He saw beneath high-piled black hair a very fair, very soft, very clever face, bright-red lips like a newly opened fig, eyebrows well tended and painted in the form of high arches, dark eyes clever and alert, a long, fair neck emerging from the green-and-gold outer garment, fair hands at rest, long and narrow, with wide gold bracelets at the wrists.

---

[8] A sex position described in the *Kamasutra:* the man stands upright while the woman stands on his feet, hoists herself up, and wraps herself around him. See "*Kamasutra*" in the Glossary.

Siddhartha saw how beautiful she was, and his heart rejoiced. He made a low bow when the chair came near him, and, straightening up again, he looked at the fair, lovely face; for a moment he read the clever eyes with the high arches above them, inhaled a breath of fragrance that he did not recognize. The beautiful woman, smiling, nodded for a moment, then disappeared into the grove, her servants following.

"And so," Siddhartha thought, "I am entering this town with a favorable omen." He was tempted to walk right into the grove, but he thought it over and only then became aware of how the servants and maids had looked at him at the entrance, how contemptuously, how distrustfully, how distantly.

"I am still a samana," he thought, "still an ascetic and mendicant. I cannot remain this way, this way I shall be unable to enter the grove." And he laughed.

He asked the next person who came his way about the grove and that woman's name, and he learned that it was the grove of Kamala, the renowned courtesan, and that, in addition to the grove, she owned a house in town.

Then he entered the town. Now he had an aim.

Pursuing his aim, he let himself be engulfed by the town; he floated on the current of the lanes; he remained standing on the squares; he rested on the stone steps by the river. Toward evening he made friends with a barber's assistant whom he had seen working in the shade of an archway, whom he ran across again praying in a temple of Vishnu, and whom he told stories concerning Vishnu and Lakshmi. That night he slept near the boats by the river, and early in the morning, before the first customers came to his shop, he had the barber's assistant shave off his beard and cut his hair, then had his hair combed and anointed with fine oil. Next he went to bathe in the river.

Late in the afternoon, when the beautiful Kamala approached her grove in her sedan chair, Siddhartha was standing at the entrance; he bowed and received the courtesan's greeting. But he beckoned to the servant who was last in line, asking him to announce to his mistress that a young Brahman wished to speak with her. After a while the servant returned, invited the waiting man to follow him, silently led the man following him into a pavilion where Kamala lay on a day bed, and left him alone with her.

"Were you not already standing there yesterday to greet me?" asked Kamala.

"Yes, I already saw you and greeted you yesterday."

"But were you not wearing a beard yesterday, and long hair, and dust in your hair?"

"You observed well, you saw everything. You saw Siddhartha, the

Brahman's son, who left his home to become a samana, and was a samana for three years. But now I have abandoned that path and have come to this town; and the first person who met me, even before I entered the town, was you. I have come to tell you that, O Kamala! You are the first woman to whom Siddhartha has spoken without standing with downcast eyes. Never again shall I lower my eyes when a beautiful woman meets me."

Kamala smiled and played with her peacock-feather fan. And she asked: "And Siddhartha has visited me merely to tell me that?"

"To tell you that, and to thank you for being so beautiful. And, if it does not displease you, Kamala, I would like to ask you to be my friend and instructress, for I still know nothing of the art in which you are an expert."

At that point Kamala laughed out loud.

"My friend, I have never had a samana come to me from the forest and want to learn from me! I have never had a samana come to me with long hair and in an old, torn loincloth! Many young men visit me, and there are Brahmans' sons among them, too, but they come in fine clothes, they come in elegant shoes, they have perfumed hair and money in their purses. That, samana, is what the young men are like who visit me."

Siddhartha said: "I am already beginning to learn from you. Even yesterday I already learned something. I have already removed my beard, combed my hair, and put oil on my hair. It is only a little that I still lack, excellent woman: elegant clothes, elegant shoes, money in my purse. Let me tell you, Siddhartha has set his mind on things more difficult than such trifles, and has attained them. How should I not attain what I set my mind on yesterday: to be your friend and to learn the joys of love from you! You will find me a quick learner, Kamala; I have learned more difficult things than what you are to teach me. And so, now: Siddhartha does not satisfy you as he is, with oil on his hair, but without clothes, without shoes, without money?"

Laughing, Kamala cried: "No, my good man, he still does not satisfy me! He must have clothes, handsome clothes, and shoes, good-looking shoes, and a lot of money in his purse, and gifts for Kamala. Now do you know, samana from the forest? Have you paid close attention?"

"Yes, I have paid close attention!" cried Siddhartha. "How could I fail to pay attention to words from such lips! Your mouth is like a newly opened fig, Kamala. My lips are red and fresh, too; they will suit yours, you will see.—But tell me, beautiful Kamala, are you not at all afraid of the samana from the forest, who has come to learn love?"

"Why, then, should I be afraid of a samana, a stupid samana from the forest, who has come from the jackals and does not yet know what women are?"

"Oh, he is strong, the samana, and afraid of nothing. He could take you by force, pretty girl. He could rob you. He could hurt you."

"No, samana, I am not afraid of that. Has a samana or a Brahman ever been afraid that someone might come, grab him, and rob him of his scholarship, his piety, and his wisdom? No, because they are his very own, and he imparts only as much of them as he wishes, and to whom he wishes. It is the same, exactly the same, with Kamala, too, and with the joys of love. Kamala's lips are beautiful and red, but try to kiss them against Kamala's will, and not a drop of sweetness will you have from them, although they are able to grant so much sweetness! You are a quick learner, Siddhartha, so learn this as well: Love can be won by begging, it can be bought, received as a gift, found on the street, but it cannot be stolen. You have hatched out a useless plan there. No, it would be a pity if a handsome young man like you wanted to attack things in such a wrong way."

Siddhartha bowed with a smile. "It would be a pity, Kamala, how right you are! It would be a terrible pity. No, not a drop of sweetness shall I lose from your lips, nor you from mine! So this is how it stands: Siddhartha will return when he has what he now lacks: clothes, shoes, money. But tell me, lovely Kamala, can you give me another small piece of advice?"

"Advice? Why not? Who would not be glad to give advice to a poor, ignorant samana who has come from the jackals in the forest?"

"Dear Kamala, then advise me: where should I go to find those three things as quickly as possible?"

"My friend, many people would like to know that. You must do what you have learned, and receive money for it, and clothes and shoes. There is no other way for a poor man to come into money. Well, what can you do?"

"I can think. I can wait. I can fast."

"Nothing else?"

"Nothing. Oh, yes, I can also compose poetry. Will you give me a kiss for a poem?"

"Yes, I will, if I like your poem. How does it go?"

After reflecting for a moment, Siddhartha uttered these verses:

"Into her shady grove stepped Kamala,
 At the entrance to the grove stood the tanned samana.
 When he caught sight of the lotus blossom,
 He made a low bow, and Kamala thanked him with a smile.
 'More lovely,' thought the young man, 'than to sacrifice to the gods,
 'More lovely it is to sacrifice to the beautiful Kamala.'"

Kamala clapped her hands loudly so that her golden arm rings clinked.

"Your verses are beautiful, tan samana, and truly I lose nothing if I give you a kiss for them."

She drew him over to her with her eyes, he lowered his face to hers, and placed his lips on those lips that were like a newly opened fig. Kamala gave him a long kiss, and in deep amazement Siddhartha felt that she was teaching him, that she was wise, that she dominated him, repulsed him, and lured him on; and that, behind this first kiss, there was a long, well-organized, and well-tested series of kisses, each one different, still awaiting him. Breathing deeply, he stood there, at that moment as astonished as a child at the wealth of knowledge and things worth learning that revealed itself to his eyes.

"Your verses are very beautiful!" Kamala cried. "If I were rich, I would give you gold coins for them. But you will find it hard to earn as much money as you need with verses. For you need a lot of money if you wish to be Kamala's friend."

"The way you can kiss, Kamala!" Siddhartha stammered.

"Yes, I am good at it, and so I have no lack of clothes, shoes, armbands, and every beautiful thing. But what will become of you? Can you do nothing but think and fast and compose poems?"

"I also know the sacrificial chants," said Siddhartha, "but I shall not sing them anymore. I also know magic charms, but I shall not pronounce them anymore. I have read the scriptures—"

"Stop there!" Kamala interrupted him. "You can read? And write?"

"Of course I can. Many people can."

"Most people cannot. I cannot, either. It is very good that you can read and write, very good. You will still be able to use the magic charms, too."

At that moment a maid came running in and whispered a piece of news in her mistress' ear.

"I am receiving a visit!" Kamala cried. "Vanish at once, Siddhartha; no one must see you here, mind that! Tomorrow I shall see you again."

But she ordered the maid to give the pious Brahman a white outer garment. Without knowing what was happening to him, Siddhartha found himself being dragged away by the maid, taken to a garden house by roundabout paths, presented with an outer garment, led into the bushes, and urgently admonished to get out of the grove at once without being seen.

He contentedly did as he was told. Accustomed to the forest, he made his way out of the grove and over the hedge noiselessly. Contentedly he returned to town, carrying the rolled-up garment under his arm. In an inn where travelers stayed, he took up a stand near the door, silently asked for food, and silently accepted a piece of rice cake. "Perhaps as soon as tomorrow," he thought, "I shall no longer ask anyone for food."

Suddenly pride flared up in him. He was no longer a samana, it was no longer fitting for him to beg. He gave the rice cake to a dog and remained without food.

"The life that people lead in the world here is simple," Siddhartha thought. "It has no difficulties. Everything was difficult, toilsome, and, when you come down to it, hopeless while I was still a samana. Now everything is easy, easy as the lessons in kissing that Kamala is giving me. I need clothes and money, nothing else; those are minor, nearby goals that do not disturb anyone's sleep."

He had found out long before where Kamala's town house was, and he showed up there on the following day.

"Things are going well!" she called to him. "You are expected at Kamaswami's; he is the wealthiest merchant in town. If he likes you, he will take you into his service. Be clever, tan samana. I have arranged it for other people to tell him about you. Be friendly to him, he is very powerful. But do not be too modest! I do not want you to become his servant; you are to become his equal, or else I shall not be satisfied with you. Kamaswami is beginning to grow old and comfort-loving. If he likes you, he will entrust many things to you."

Siddhartha thanked her and laughed, and when she heard that he had eaten nothing that day or the day before, she had bread and fruit brought in, and invited him to eat.

"You have been lucky," she said while saying good-bye; "one door after the other is opening up for you. Now, how is that? Do you possess some magic?"

Siddhartha said: "Yesterday I told you that I knew how to think, to wait, and to fast; but you thought that it was all useless. But it is useful in many ways, Kamala, you will see. You will see that the stupid samanas in the forest learn many fine things and can do a lot that you cannot. The day before yesterday I was still a disheveled beggar; yesterday I already kissed Kamala; and soon I shall be a merchant and have money and all those things that you value."

"Well, yes," she admitted. "But what would your situation be if not for me? What would you be if Kamala were not helping you?"

"Dear Kamala," Siddhartha said, rising to his full height, "when I visited you in your grove, I took the first step. It was my intention to learn love from that most beautiful woman. From the moment that I formulated that intention, I also knew that I would carry it out. I knew that you would help me, I already knew it when you gave me that first look at the entrance to the grove."

"But if I had not been willing?"

"You *were* willing. Look, Kamala: if you throw a stone into the water, it hastens to the bottom by the quickest route. Thus it is when Siddhartha has a goal or an intention. Siddhartha does not act; he waits, he thinks, he fasts, but he pierces through the things of this world as the stone goes through the water, without performing any action, without bestirring himself; he is drawn, he lets himself fall. His goal draws him toward itself, because he admits nothing into his soul that could oppose that goal. That is what Siddhartha learned from the samanas. That is what fools call magic, in the belief that it is brought about by demons. Nothing is brought about by demons, there are no demons. Anyone can work magic, anyone can attain his goals, if he can think, if he can wait, if he can fast."

Kamala listened to him. She loved his voice, she loved the look in his eyes.

"It may be as you say, my friend," she said softly. "But it may also be that good fortune comes Siddhartha's way because he is a handsome man, because women like his eyes."

Siddhartha said good-bye with a kiss. "Let it be so, my instructress. May you always like my eyes, may good fortune always come to me from you!"

With the Child-People

Siddhartha went to the merchant Kamaswami; he was shown into a wealthy home; servants led him past expensive tapestries into a room where he was to wait for the master of the house.

In came Kamaswami, a lively, limber man with heavily graying hair, with very clever, prudent eyes, with lips that betokened desire. Host and guest greeted each other in friendly fashion.

"I have been told," the merchant began, "that you are a Brahman, a learned man, but that you are seeking service with a merchant. Is it because you have fallen on hard times, Brahman, that you are seeking service?"

"No," said Siddhartha, "I have not fallen on hard times and I have never known hard times. Let me inform you that I have come from among the samanas, with whom I lived for a long period."

"If you are coming from the samanas, how can you not be in need? Are not the samanas completely without possessions?"

"I am without possessions," Siddhartha said, "if that is what you mean. Certainly, I am without possessions. But I am so voluntarily, and so I am not in need."

"But what do you expect to live on if you have no possessions?"

"I have never yet thought about it, sir. I have been without possessions for over three years and I have never thought about what I would live on."

"So you lived on the possessions of other people."

"Presumably so. Surely, a merchant, too, lives on other people's wealth."

"Well said. But he does not take people's money from them for nothing; he gives them his merchandise for it."

"Apparently that is actually the case. Everyone takes, everyone gives, such is life."

"But permit me: if you have no possessions, what do you expect to give?"

"Everyone gives what he has. The warrior gives his strength, the merchant gives his wares, the teacher his teachings, the farmer his rice, the fisherman his fish."

"Very good. And now, what is it that you have to give? What is it that you have learned, that you are able to do?"

"I can think. I can wait. I can fast."

"And that is all?"

"I believe that that is all!"

"And what good is that? For example, fasting—what is it good for?"

"It is very good, sir. If a person has nothing to eat, then to fast is the cleverest thing he can do. For example, if Siddhartha had not learned how to fast, this very day he would have to accept any position whatsoever, either with you or anywhere else, because hunger would compel him to. But, this way, Siddhartha can wait calmly, he knows no impatience, he knows no distress, he can let himself be besieged by hunger for a long time and can laugh at the situation. That, sir, is what fasting is good for."

"You are right, samana. Wait a moment."

Kamaswami went out and returned with a scroll, which he handed to his guest, asking: "Can you read this?"

Siddhartha looked at the scroll, on which a sales contract was written, and began to read its contents aloud.

"Excellent," said Kamaswami. "And do you mind writing something for me on this sheet?"

He gave him a sheet and a stylus; Siddhartha wrote and gave back the sheet.

Kamaswami read: "Writing is good, thinking is better. Cleverness is good, patience is better."

"You know how to write extremely well," the merchant said approvingly. "We will have much more to say to each other. For today I ask you to be my guest and take up residence in this house."

Siddhartha thanked him and accepted the position, and thereafter lived in the merchant's house. He was brought clothes and shoes, and every day a servant prepared his bath. Twice a day a copious meal was served, but Siddhartha ate only once a day; moreover, he ate no meat and he drank no wine. Kamaswami told him about his business, showed him merchandise and storehouses, showed him ledgers. Siddhartha became acquainted with many new things, listening carefully but saying little. And, mindful of what Kamala had said, he never subordinated himself to the merchant, but compelled him to treat him as an equal, indeed as more than an equal. Kamaswami ran his business conscientiously and often passionately, but Siddhartha regarded it all as a game, the rules of which he strove to learn accurately, but the substance of which did not touch his heart.

Before he had been in Kamaswami's house very long, he was already taking part in his host's dealings. But every day, at the time she designated, he visited the beautiful Kamala, wearing handsome clothes and elegant shoes, and soon he even brought along gifts for her. Her clever red lips taught him much. Her delicate, supple hands taught him much. Still a boy when it came to love and, moreover, inclined to plunge into his pleasure blindly and insatiably as into a bottomless pit, he learned thoroughly from her that pleasure cannot be taken without giving pleasure in return, and that every gesture, every caress, every touch, every look, every inch of the body, has its secret, the awakening of which affords happiness to the knowing person. She taught him that lovers should not part after a love fest without admiring each other, without feeling they have been conquered as much as they themselves have conquered, so that neither one of them suffers from satiety, boredom, or the unpleasant sensation of having abused the other or having been abused. He spent marvelous hours with the beautiful, clever artiste; he became her pupil, her lover, her friend. Here, with Kamala, lay the value and meaning of his present life, not in Kamaswami's commerce.

The merchant entrusted to him the writing of important letters and contracts, and became accustomed to discussing every important matter with him. He soon saw that Siddhartha understood little about rice or wool, ship transport or business, but that he had a knack for what he was doing, and that Siddhartha surpassed him, the merchant, in calmness and equanimity and in the art of listening and the accurate evaluation of strangers. "This Brahman," he said to a friend, "is no real merchant and will never become one, he is never passionately involved in the business. But he possesses the secret of those people to whom success comes all on its own, whether because a lucky star was shining when they were born, or through magic, or through something he learned from the samanas. He always appears to be merely playing with business, it never completely occupies his mind, it never dominates him, he is never afraid of failure, he never frets over a loss."

The friend advised the merchant: "Give him a third of the profits from the deals he makes for you, but let him also lose the same percentage when the business suffers a loss. That way he will become more enthusiastic."

Kamaswami followed the advice. But Siddhartha was not much concerned about it. If he made a profit, he accepted it with indifference; if he suffered a loss, he laughed, saying: "Just look, this turned out badly!"

It really seemed as if business did not matter to him. On one occasion, he traveled to a village to purchase a sizable rice crop there. When he arrived, however, the rice had already been sold to another dealer. Nevertheless, Siddhartha remained in that village for many days; he treated the farmers to meals, he gave their children copper coins, he was a guest at a wedding, and returned from his trip highly satisfied. Kamaswami reproached him for not having come back at once, for wasting time and money. Siddhartha replied: "Stop scolding, my dear friend! Nothing has ever yet been achieved by scolding. If there has been a loss, then let me bear the loss. I am very satisfied with this trip. I met all sorts of people, I made friends with a Brahman, I dandled children on my knee, farmers showed me their fields, no one took me for a businessman."

"That is all very fine!" Kamaswami cried indignantly. "But in reality you *are* a businessman, I should think! Or were you just taking a pleasure trip?"

"Of course," Siddhartha laughed. "Of course, I was taking a pleasure trip. Why else should I travel? I got to know people and places, I enjoyed friendliness and trust, I found friendship. Look, dear friend, if I had been Kamaswami, as soon as I saw that my deal was nullified, I would have come back again in haste, filled with vexation, and my time and money would really have been lost. But, this way, I had a good time, I learned things, I tasted joy, and I harmed neither myself nor others through vexation or through hastiness. And if I ever go back there again, perhaps to buy a future crop, or for any other reason, friendly people will receive me in a friendly and cheerful way, and I shall applaud myself for not having exhibited haste or displeasure on the former occasion. So let it go, my friend, and do not do yourself harm by scolding! When the day comes on which you see, 'This Siddhartha is doing me damage,' then just say the word and Siddhartha will go his way. But till then let us be satisfied with each other."

Just as futile were the merchant's attempts to convince Siddhartha that he was eating his, Kamaswami's, bread. Siddhartha was eating his own bread; or, rather, both of them were eating other people's bread, everybody's bread. Siddhartha never lent an ear to Kamaswami's worries, and Kamaswami worried a lot. If a business deal in progress threatened to be unsuccessful, if a shipment seemed to be lost, if a debtor seemed unable to pay, Kamaswami was never able to convince his associate that it was a useful thing to utter words of concern or anger, to knit one's brows, or to lose sleep. When Kamaswami, on one occasion, rebuked him, saying he had learned everything he knew from him, he replied: "Please do not pull my leg with that sort of joke! I have learned from you how much a basket of fish costs, and how much interest can be demanded for a loan of money. That is your corpus of knowledge. But I did not learn how to think from you, my dear Kamaswami; it would be better if you tried to learn that from me."

In truth, his heart was not in commerce. Business was good for making money that he could spend on Kamala, and he made much more at it than he needed. Otherwise, Siddhartha's interests and curiosity were only about people, whose business dealings, artisanry, worries, entertainments, and follies had previously been as foreign to him and remote from him as the moon. No matter how easy it was for him to talk to everyone, to live with everyone, to learn from everyone, he was nevertheless fully aware that there was something that set him apart from them, and that this alienating factor was his experience as a samana. He saw people going through life like children or animals, and he both loved and looked down on that way of life. He saw them laboring, suffering, and growing gray for the sake of things that seemed to him not at all worth that price: for money, for petty pleasures, for petty honors. He saw them scold and insult one another, he saw them complain about pains that a samana smiles at, and suffer from privations that a samana fails to notice.

He was open to everything these people could give him. He welcomed the merchant who offered to sell him linen, he welcomed the debtor who asked him for a loan, he welcomed the beggar who told him the history of his poverty for a full hour, although he was not half as poor as any samana. He treated wealthy foreign merchants just as he treated the servant who shaved him, or the street vendor, whom he allowed to cheat him out of small change when he bought plantains. When Kamaswami came to him to complain about his worries or to reproach him over some business deal, he listened inquisitively and serenely, was amazed at him, tried to understand him, let him have his own way to some extent, just as much as he considered indispensable, and then turned away from him and on to the next person who wanted him. And many people came to him, many to do business with him, many to cheat him, many to sound him out, many to call upon his sympathy, many to hear his advice. He gave advice, he offered sympathy, he made gifts, he allowed himself to be cheated a little; and this entire game, and the passion with which all people played this game, occupied his thoughts just as much as the gods and the *Brahman* had occupied them in the past.

At times he heard, deep in his heart, a very faint, still voice that quietly admonished him, quietly lamented, so it could barely be perceived. At such times he became aware for an hour or so that he was leading a strange life, that he was doing nothing but playing a mere game, that although he might be serene and might sometimes feel joy, true life was nevertheless passing him by without touching him. The way a ball player plays with the ball, so did he play with his business, with the people around him, watching them, finding amusement in them; his heart, the wellspring of his being, was not in it. The wellspring flowed elsewhere, as if far from him; it flowed on and on invisibly, and had nothing more to do with his life. And a few times he was alarmed at these thoughts and wished that it might be vouchsafed to him, as well, to take part in all the childlike activity of each day passionately and wholeheartedly, really to live, really to act, really to enjoy and to live instead of merely standing by in that way like a spectator.

But he went on visiting the beautiful Kamala; he learned the art of love; he practiced the cult of pleasure, in which more than anywhere else giving and taking become one and the same; he chatted with her, learned from her, gave her advice, received advice. She understood him better than Govinda had formerly understood him; she was more like him.

On one occasion, he said to her: "You are like me, you are different from most people. You are Kamala, nothing else, and within you there is a tranquillity and refuge, in which you can take shelter at any time and be at home with yourself, just as I can, too. Not many people have that, and yet everybody could have it."

"Not all people are clever," Kamala said.

"No," Siddhartha said, "that is not the reason. Kamaswami is just as clever as I am, and yet has no refuge within himself. Others have it, although they have the minds of little children. Most people, Kamala, are like a falling leaf, which drifts and turns in the air, and sways, and zigzags to the ground. But others, just a few, are like stars; they travel a fixed route, no wind reaches them; their law and their route lie within themselves. Among all the many learned men and samanas I have known, one man of this type had attained perfection; I can never forget him. I mean Gotama, the Sublime One, who proclaims that doctrine. A thousand disciples hear his teachings every day, and follow his regulations every hour, but they are all falling leaves; they do not possess the doctrine and the law within themselves."

Kamala studied him, smiling. "You are talking about him again," she said; "again you are thinking like a samana."

Siddhartha was silent, and they played the game of love, one of the thirty or forty different varieties of the game that Kamala knew. Her body was as lithe as a jaguar's[9] or as a hunter's bow; a man who had learned love from her was acquainted with many pleasures, many secrets. For a long while she sported with Siddhartha, luring him on, repulsing him, forcing his will, encircling him, enjoying his mastery, until he was vanquished and lay exhausted at her side.

The hetaera leaned over him, taking a long look at his face, at his eyes that had grown weary.

She said reflectively, "You are the best lover I have seen. You are stronger than others, more supple, more willing. You have learned my art well, Siddhartha. Sometime when I am older, I want to bear your child. And yet, dear, you have remained a samana; and yet, you do not love me, you do not love anyone. Am I not right?"

"It may be so," said Siddhartha wearily. "I am like you. You do not love anyone, either—otherwise, how could you practice love as an art? Perhaps people of our kind are unable to love. The child-people can; that is their secret."

Samsara

For a long time Siddhartha had lived the life of the world and its pleasures without really belonging to it. His senses, which he had mortified in his ardent samana years, had reawakened; he had tasted wealth, had tasted sensual delights, had tasted power; and yet, for a long time he had still remained a samana in his heart; clever Kamala had realized that correctly. It was always the art of thinking, waiting, and fasting that directed his life; the people of the world, the child-people, had always still remained foreign to him, just as he was foreign to them.

The years sped by; cushioned by prosperity, Siddhartha barely felt their passing. He had become wealthy; for some time he had had a house of his own, his own servants, and a garden in the suburbs by the river. People liked him; they came to him when they needed money or advice; but no one was close to him except Kamala.

That lofty, clear sensation of wakefulness he had once experienced

---

[9] An odd comparison in the context of the novel; the jaguar is a New World animal.

in the prime of his youth, in the days after Gotama's preaching, after his separation from Govinda, that tense feeling of expectancy, that proud independence from teachings and teachers, that pliant readiness to hear the divine voice in his own heart, had gradually become just a memory, it had been transitory. Distantly and quietly murmured the sacred wellspring that had once been nearby, that had once resounded within himself. To be sure, for a long time he had retained much of what he had learned from the samanas, from Gotama, from his father the Brahman: a moderate way of life, pleasure in thinking, hours of concentration, secret knowledge of the self, of the eternal "I" that is neither body nor consciousness. He had retained much of that, but one thing after another had been submerged and had become covered with dust. Just as a potter's wheel, once set in motion, still turns for a long time and only slowly slackens and comes to rest, thus in Siddhartha's soul the wheel of asceticism, the wheel of thought, the wheel of discernment, had kept on turning for some time, and was still turning, but turning slowly and hesitantly, and it was close to stopping. Slowly, the way that moisture penetrates a dying tree stump, slowly filling it and making it rot, the world and indolence had penetrated Siddhartha's soul; slowly it filled his soul, making it heavy, making it weary, lulling it to sleep. In compensation for that, his senses had become alert; they had learned a great deal, experienced a great deal.

Siddhartha had learned how to conduct business, how to exercise power over people, how to enjoy women; he had learned to wear beautiful clothes, to give orders to servants, to bathe in scented water. He had learned to eat delicately and carefully prepared dishes, even fish, even meat and poultry, spices and sweets, and to drink wine, which makes you indolent and forgetful. He had learned to play dice and chess, to watch dancing girls, to be carried in a sedan chair, to sleep on a soft bed. But still he had always set himself apart from the rest, feeling superior to them; he had always watched them with a little mockery, with a little mocking contempt, with precisely that contempt which a samana always feels for worldlings. Whenever Kamaswami felt unwell, whenever he was peevish, whenever he felt insulted, whenever he was plagued by his business worries, Siddhartha had always looked on mockingly. Only slowly and imperceptibly, with the passing harvest seasons and rainy seasons, had his mockery grown wearier, had his superiority become quieter. Only slowly, amid his growing riches, had Siddhartha himself taken on something of the nature of the child-people, something of their childlikeness and of their anxiety. And yet he envied them; he envied them more, the more he became like them. He envied them for the one thing that he lacked and they had, for the importance they were able to attach to their life, for the passionate quality of their joys and fears, for the anxious but sweet happiness of their perpetual loving. These people were always in love: with themselves or with women; they loved their children, they loved honor or money, plans or hopes. But it was this, precisely this, that he did not learn from them, this childlike joy and childlike folly; what he did learn from them was precisely what he found unpleasant and had contempt for. It occurred more and more frequently that on the morning after an evening of partying he lay in bed for a long time, feeling stupid and tired. He would become peevish and impatient when Kamaswami bored him with his worries. He would laugh too loud when he lost at dice. His face was still cleverer and more intellectual than other people's, but it seldom laughed, and, one by one, it acquired those lines so frequently found in rich people's faces, those lines of dissatisfaction, sickliness, bad temper, indolence, lovelessness. Slowly the mental malady of the rich was taking hold of him.

Like a veil, like a thin mist, weariness descended upon Siddhartha, slowly, every day a little denser, every month a little more opaque, every year a little heavier. Just as a new garment becomes old with time, loses its beautiful color with time, gets stained, gets creased, gets frayed at the seams, and begins to show worn-out, threadbare places here and there, thus had Siddhartha's new life, which he had begun after his separation from Govinda, become old; thus, with the fleeting years, it was losing its color and brightness; thus creases and stains gathered on it; and, concealed below, but already showing through in their ugliness here and there, disappointment and disgust lay in wait. Siddhartha did not notice this. He only noticed that that bright, confident voice within him, that had once awakened in him and had constantly directed him in his most brilliant days, had become taciturn.

The world had entrapped him, pleasure, covetousness, indolence, and finally even the vice he had always despised and scorned most, as being the most foolish: avarice. Property, too, possessions and wealth had finally entrapped him; they were no longer a game or toy to him, but had become a chain and a burden. Siddhartha had fallen into this ultimate, vilest dependency by way of an unusual, deceitful path: through dice playing. For, from the time he had ceased in his heart to be a samana, Siddhartha had begun to gamble for money and expensive things with increasing fury and passion, whereas earlier he had only been participating, smiling and unconcerned, in a custom of the child-people. He was a dreaded player; not many people dared to oppose him, his stakes were so high and reckless. He played out of his heart's distress; to lose and squander his wretched money gave him an angry joy; in no other way could he show more clearly and scornfully his contempt for wealth, the false idol of the merchant class. And so he played for high stakes, ruthlessly, hating himself, scorning himself; he raked in thousands, threw away thousands, lost money, lost jewelry, lost a country villa, won again, lost again. He loved the fear, that awful, oppressive fear that he felt during a dice game, while he was anxious over his high stakes; he strove to renew that fear again and again, to keep intensifying it, to keep titillating it, for only in this sensation did he still feel something like happiness, something like intoxication, something like a heightened form of life, in the midst of his surfeited, tepid, dull existence. And after every big loss he thought about new wealth, he pursued his business interests more enthusiastically, he was firmer in forcing his debtors to pay up, because he wanted to continue gambling, he wanted to continue squandering wealth and showing his contempt for it. Siddhartha lost his calmness when the dice went against him; he lost his patience with those slow to pay him, lost his kindly feeling for beggars, lost his pleasure in giving away or lending money to those who asked for it. Although he would lose ten thousand on a single cast and laugh over it, he became stricter and pettier in his business dealings; he sometimes dreamed of money at night! And every time he awoke from that hateful enchantment, every time he saw in the mirror on his bedroom wall how much his face had aged and grown uglier, every time he was seized by shame and disgust, he ran farther away; he fled to new games of chance, he fled to mind-numbing sensual pleasures and wine, and from there back to the urge to accumulate and gain. In this meaningless cycle he ran himself weary, ran himself old, ran himself sick.

Then, one night, a dream warned him. He had spent the evening hours with Kamala, in her beautiful pleasure garden. They had sat beneath the trees, talking, and Kamala had spoken thoughtful words, words behind which sadness and weariness lay concealed. She had asked him to tell her about Gotama, and she could not hear enough about him, how pure his eyes had been, how calm and beautiful his lips, how kindly his smile, how peaceful his walk. He had had to give her a long account of the sublime Buddha, and Kamala had sighed, saying: "Sometime, maybe soon, I, too, shall follow this Buddha. I shall make him a gift of my pleasure garden, and shall take refuge in his Law." But, after that, she had incited him and had chained him to her in love play with painful ardor, with bites and with tears, as if she wanted just once more to squeeze the last drop of sweetness out of this vain, transitory pleasure. Never had it become so unusually clear to Siddhartha how closely sex is related to death. Afterward he had lain at her side, and Kamala's face had been near him, and below her eyes and at the corners of her mouth he had read more clearly than ever before an anxious message, written in fine lines, in light wrinkles, a message reminding him of autumn and old age—for Siddhartha himself, who was only in his forties, had already noticed gray hairs among his black hair here and there. Weariness was written on Kamala's beautiful face, weariness from traveling a long path that has no happy goal, weariness and the onset of fading, and an anxiety that was kept secret, not yet uttered, perhaps not yet even conscious: fear of old age, fear of the autumn, fear of the necessity of dying. He had taken leave of her with a sigh, his soul filled with aversion and filled with concealed anxiety.

Then Siddhartha had spent the night at home with dancing girls and wine; he had played the part of a superior man vis-à-vis his peers, although he no longer was one; he had drunk much wine and had gone to bed long after midnight, weary and yet agitated, close to tears and despair; for a long time he had tried in vain to fall asleep, his heart full of a misery that he thought he could no longer bear, full of a disgust that he felt permeating him like the tepid, repellent taste of the wine, like the oversweet, monotonous music, like the too simpering smiles of the dancing girls and the oversweet fragrance of their hair and breasts. But, more than with anything else, he was disgusted with himself, with his scented hair, with the smell of wine from his mouth, with the flabby tiredness and irritability of his skin. Just as someone who has eaten or drunk too much vomits it out again in great discomfort but nevertheless is glad of the relief, thus the insomniac wished he could rid himself of these pleasures, of these habits, of this whole pointless life, and of himself, in one enormous surge of nausea. He had not dropped off to sleep until the morning light and the first flurry of activity on the street in front of his town house; for a few moments he had achieved semiconsciousness, a foretaste of sleep. During these moments he had a dream:

Kamala owned a small, rare songbird that she kept in a golden cage. It was this bird he dreamt about. In his dream, this bird, which usually always sang at the morning hour, remained silent; and, since this attracted his attention, he stepped up to the cage and looked in; the little bird was dead, and lay rigid on the floor of the cage. He took it out, weighed it in his hand for a moment, and then threw it away, out into the lane; and, at the same moment, he received a terrible fright, and his heart ached as if he had cast away everything valuable and good from himself together with that dead bird.

Starting up out of that dream, he felt hemmed in by a profound sadness. It appeared to him that he had been living his life in a worthless way, worthless and pointless; nothing alive, nothing in the least way valuable or worth keeping, had remained in his hands. He stood there alone and empty like a shipwrecked man on the shore.

Gloomily Siddhartha went to a pleasure garden he owned, locked the gate, sat down beneath a mango tree, felt death in his heart and terror in his bosom; he sat there and physically felt a dying, fading, and ending within him. Gradually he collected his thoughts and mentally retraced the entire course of his life, from the very first days he was able to recall. When had he ever experienced happiness, felt true bliss? Oh, yes, he had experienced it several times. As a boy he had tasted it when he had elicited praise from the Brahmans, when, far surpassing the others of his age, he had distinguished himself in reciting the holy verses, in disputations with the learned men, as an assistant at the sacrifices. At such times he had felt in his heart: "A path lies before you to which you are called, the gods are waiting for you." And, then, as a young man, when the ever-elusive goal of all reflective thought had plucked him out of the mass of all the other contenders and had borne him upward; when he was painfully struggling for the meaning of *Brahman*, when every bit of knowledge he acquired merely kindled fresh thirst in him—there too, amid his thirst, amid his pain, he had had the same feeling: "Onward! Onward! You have a calling!" He had heard that voice when he had left home and chosen a samana's life, and again when he had departed from the samanas and gone to that Perfect One, and then when he had departed from him and gone into the unknown. How long it was now since he had heard that voice, how long since he had scaled any heights; how evenly and monotonously his journey had gone on, many long years without a lofty goal, knowing no thirst or elevation of spirit, contented with petty pleasures and yet never satisfied! For all these years, without knowing it, he had labored and longed to become a human being like all these others, like these children, and all that time his life had been much more wretched and poor than theirs, because their goals were not his, nor their worries; in fact, this whole world of Kamaswami-people had been just a game to him, a dance that you watch, a comedy. Only Kamala had been dear to him, had had value for him—but did she still? Did he still need her, or she him? Were they not playing a game that had no end? Was it necessary to go on living for that? No, it was not necessary! This game was called *samsara*, a game for children, a game it might be pleasant to play once, twice, ten times—but over and over again?

Then Siddhartha knew that the game was over, that he could not play it anymore. He shuddered all over his body, and inside him, and he felt that something had died.

That whole day he sat beneath the mango tree, recalling his father, recalling Govinda, recalling Gotama. Had it been necessary to abandon them in order to become a Kamaswami? He was still sitting there when night fell. When he looked up and caught sight of the stars, he thought: "Here I am sitting beneath my mango tree in my pleasure garden." He smiled slightly—was it necessary, then, was it proper, was it not just a foolish game, for him to own a mango tree and a garden?

He called it quits with that, as well; that, too, died within him. He got up, said good-bye to the mango tree, good-bye to the pleasure garden. Since he had spent the whole day without eating, he felt a ravenous hunger, and recalled his house in town, his room and bed, the table laden with food. He smiled wearily, shook himself, and said good-bye to those things.

In the same hour of the night, Siddhartha abandoned his garden, abandoned the town, and never returned. For a long time Kamaswami had him searched for, believing he had fallen into the hands of highwaymen. Kamala did not have him searched for. When she learned that Siddhartha had disappeared, she was not surprised. Had she not always expected it? Was he not a samana, a homeless man, a wanderer? And she had felt this most strongly the last time they were together; and, amid the pain of her loss, she was glad that, on that last occasion, she had still drawn him so lovingly to her heart, that she had once again felt so fully possessed and permeated by him.

When she received the first news of Siddhartha's disappearance, she went to the window where she kept a rare songbird in a golden cage. She opened the cage door, took the bird out, and let it fly away. For a long time she watched it go, that flying bird. From that day on, she accepted no more visits and kept her house locked up. But after a while she became aware that her last meeting with Siddhartha had left her pregnant.

By the River

Siddhartha wandered through the forest, already far from the town; he knew only this: that he could not return, that the life he had now been leading for many years was over and done with, that he had tasted and drained it to the surfeiting point. Dead was the songbird of which he had dreamed. Dead was the bird in his heart. He was tightly entangled in *samsara*; he had imbibed disgust and death from all sides, as a sponge soaks up water until it is full. He was full of distaste, full of misery, full of death; there was nothing more in the world that could entice him, gladden him, console him.

He ardently wished to know nothing more about himself, to enjoy repose, to be dead. If only a lightning bolt would come and kill him! If only a tiger would come and devour him! If only there were a wine, a poison, that could bring him unconsciousness, oblivion, and sleep without any more awakening! For was there any kind of filth he had not filthied himself with, any sin and folly he had not committed, any barrenness of the soul he had not burdened himself with? Was it possible to go on living? Was it possible to keep on constantly breathing in, breathing out, feeling hunger, eating again, sleeping again, lying with a woman again? Was not this cycle exhausted and terminated for him?

Siddhartha reached the wide river in the forest, the same river over which a ferryman had once taken him when he was still a young man coming from Gotama's town. By that river he halted, lingering hesitantly on its bank. Fatigue and hunger had weakened him—and, then, what reason had he to continue on, and where to, toward what goal? No, there were no longer any goals, nothing was left but the deep-seated, sorrowful longing to shake off that entire chaotic dream, to spit out that flat wine, to make an end of that pathetic, shameful life.

A tree leaned forward over the riverbank, a coconut palm. Siddhartha rested his shoulder against its trunk, placed his arm around the trunk, and looked down into the green water that continued to flow by below him. He looked down and discovered that he was totally imbued with the desire to let himself go and sink in that water. He saw a frightful void reflected in that water, corresponding to the terrible void in his soul. Yes, he had reached the end. There was nothing left for him but to obliterate himself, to shatter the abortive structure of his life, to throw it away at the feet of gods who would laugh in scorn. This was the great fit of vomiting he had longed for: death, the shattering of the mold that he hated! Let the fish devour him, that dog Siddhartha, that lunatic, that corrupt, decayed body, that flaccid, misused soul! Let the fish and crocodiles devour him, let the demons[10] tear him apart!

His features distorted, he stared into the water; seeing the reflection of his face, he spat at it. In profound weariness he detached his arm from the tree trunk and turned his body slightly so that he would fall vertically, and finally perish. His eyes closed, he was dropping to his death.

Just then, from remote regions of his soul, from past periods of his tired life, a sound ran through his mind like a flash. It was a word, a syllable, that he spoke to himself involuntarily in a slurred voice, that old word which begins and ends every Brahmanist prayer, the sacred *om*, which is equivalent in meaning to "perfection" or "the absolute." And at the moment that the sound *om* touched Siddhartha's ears, his intellect, which had fallen asleep, suddenly awakened and realized the folly of what he was doing.

Siddhartha was thoroughly frightened. So, then, things were so bad for him, he was so lost, so far astray and abandoned by all knowledge,

---

[10] Siddhartha has claimed earlier that there are no demons. Perhaps here the term is merely a poetical equivalent of the crocodiles and other deadly creatures.

that he had been able to seek death; that that wish, that childish wish, had been able to grow strong within him: to find peace by obliterating his body! What all the torment of those recent days, all his sober reflections, all his despair, had not accomplished, was accomplished by the moment when *om* penetrated his consciousness: he understood himself in his misery and his maze of error.

"*Om!*" he said to himself: "*Om!*" And once more he knew about *Brahman,* he knew about the indestructibility of life, he knew about all the divine things he had forgotten.

But this was only a moment, a lightning flash. Siddhartha sank down at the foot of the coconut palm, laid his head on the tree's roots, and sank into deep sleep.

His sleep was deep and dreamless; for a long time he had not known such sleep. When he awakened many hours later, he felt as if ten years had gone by; he heard the quiet flowing of the water; he did not know where he was or who had brought him there; he opened his eyes, and in surprise saw trees and sky above him, and remembered where he was and how he had gotten there. But this took him a long time, and the past seemed to him to lie under a veil, to be infinitely distant, infinitely far away, infinitely unimportant. All he knew was that he had left his earlier life behind (in the first moments of his return to his senses, that earlier life resembled a previous incarnation in the remote past, an early prenatal state of his present self); he knew that, filled with disgust and misery, he had even wanted to throw away his life, but that he had regained consciousness by a river, under a coconut palm, the sacred word *om* on his lips; he had then fallen asleep, and now, awake again, he was looking at the world like a new person. Softly he spoke the word *om* to himself, the word that had been in his thoughts when he fell asleep, and he felt as if all of his long sleep had been nothing but a long utterance of *om* in a state of concentration, a meditation on *om*, an immersion and total absorption into *om*, into the nameless, the absolute.

Really, what a marvelous sleep that had been! Never had sleep so refreshed him, so renewed him, so rejuvenated him! Perhaps he had really died, had perished, and was now reborn in a new shape? But no, he recognized himself, he recognized his hands and feet, he recognized the place where he was lying, he recognized that "I" in his bosom, that Siddhartha, that willful, strange man; and yet this Siddhartha was transformed, he was renewed, he was remarkably rested, remarkably awake, joyful and inquisitive.

Siddhartha sat up, whereupon he saw someone sitting opposite him, a stranger, a monk in a yellow robe, with a shaved head, in the pose of contemplation. He observed the man, who had neither hair on his head nor a beard; but he had not been observing him very long when he recognized in that monk Govinda, the friend of his youth, Govinda, who had taken refuge in the sublime Buddha. Govinda had aged, too, but his face still bore the same old features, betokening enthusiasm, loyalty, questing, anxiety. But now, when Govinda, feeling his eyes upon him, opened his own eyes and looked at him, Siddhartha saw that Govinda did not recognize him. Govinda was glad to find him awake; obviously he had been sitting there for some time waiting for him to awaken, even though he did not know him.

"I have been sleeping," Siddhartha said. "How did you get here?"

"You have been sleeping," Govinda replied. "It is not good to sleep in places like this, where there are often snakes and where the forest animals have their trails. I, sir, am a disciple of the sublime Gotama, the Buddha, the Sakyamuni, and I was wandering this way with a group of my fellows when I saw you lying asleep in a place where it is dangerous to sleep. Therefore I tried to awaken you, sir, and when I saw that your sleep was very deep, I remained behind while my friends went on, and I sat with you. And then, it seems, I fell asleep myself, I who wanted to guard you while you slept. I have done my duty badly, fatigue overpowered me. But now that you are awake, let me go so that I can overtake my brothers."

"Thank you, samana, for watching over me while I slept," Siddhartha said. "You disciples of the Sublime One are friendly. Now you may go."

"I am going, sir. May you always enjoy good health, sir."

"Thank you, samana."

Govinda made the sign of leavetaking and said: "Farewell."

"Farewell, Govinda," Siddhartha said.

The monk stopped short.

"Pardon me, sir, how do you know my name?"

Thereupon Siddhartha smiled.

"I know you, O Govinda, from your father's cottage, and from the Brahmanic school, and from the sacrifices, and from our journey to the samanas, and from the hour when you took refuge in the Sublime One in the grove of Jetavana."

"You are Siddhartha!" Govinda shouted out loud. "Now I recognize you, and I fail to understand how I did not recognize you at once. Welcome, Siddhartha, great is my joy at seeing you again."

"I, too, am pleased to see you again. You have been the guardian of my slumbers, for which I thank you again, even though I needed no guardian. Where are you headed for, my friend?"

"Nowhere in particular. We monks are always journeying, except in the rainy season; we are always proceeding from one place to another, living by our rules, proclaiming the doctrine, accepting alms, journeying farther. It is always like that. But you, Siddhartha, where are you headed for?"

Siddhartha said: "It is the same with me, too, friend, as with you. I am going nowhere in particular. I am merely journeying. I am wandering."

Govinda said: "You say you are wandering and I believe you. But forgive me, O Siddhartha, you do not look like a wanderer. You are wearing a rich man's garment, you are wearing an aristocrat's shoes, and your hair, with its fragrance of scented water, is not the hair of a wanderer, not the hair of a samana."

"Yes, my dear friend, you have observed well; your sharp eyes see everything. But I did not say I was a samana. I said I was wandering. And it is true: I am wandering."

"You are wandering," Govinda said. "But not many people go wandering in such a garment, in such shoes, with such well-groomed hair. I, who have been wandering for many years now, have never run across a wanderer of that sort."

"I believe you, my Govinda. But now, today, you have run across just such a wanderer, in such shoes, in such a garment. Remember, my dear friend: the world of created forms is transitory; transitory, extremely transitory, are our garments, and the way we do our hair, and our hair and body themselves. I am wearing a rich man's clothes, you have seen that rightly. I am wearing them because I have been a rich man, and my hair is dressed like that of worldlings and voluptuaries because I have been one."

"And now, Siddhartha, what are you now?"

"I do not know, I know no more about it than you do. I am journeying. I was a rich man and I no longer am; and what I shall be tomorrow I do not know."

"You have lost your wealth?"

"I have lost it, or it has lost me. It got away from me. The wheel of created forms turns swiftly, Govinda. Where is Siddhartha the Brahman? Where is Siddhartha the samana? Where is Siddhartha the rich man? Transitory things change swiftly, Govinda, as you know."

Govinda took a long look at the friend of his youth, with doubt in his eyes. Then he took leave of him as one takes leave of aristocrats, and went his way.

With a smile on his face Siddhartha watched him go; he still loved that loyal, anxious man. And how could he fail to love any person or any thing at this moment, at this splendid hour following his miraculous sleep, when he was permeated with *om*! This was the very nature of the enchantment that had befallen him through the *om* while sleeping: that he loved everything, that he was filled with happy love for everything he saw. And it now appeared to him that it had been his inability to love anything or anyone that had previously made him so ill.

With a smile on his face, Siddhartha watched the departing monk. His sleep had greatly strengthened him, but he had severe hunger pangs because he had not eaten for two days now, and that time was long past when he had been fortified against hunger. He remembered that time with sorrow, yet with a laugh, too. Back then, he recalled, he had boasted to Kamala of three things; he had mastered three noble, invincible arts: fasting, waiting, thinking. Those had been his possessions, his power and strength, his firm rod; in the diligent, laborious years of his youth he had learned those three arts and nothing else. And now they had deserted him; not one of them was his any longer, neither fasting, nor waiting, nor thinking. He had given them up for the sake of the most wretched things, the most transitory things, for sensual pleasure, for luxury, for wealth! His experience had really been a strange one. And now, it seemed, now he had truly become a child-person.

Siddhartha reflected on his situation. It was hard for him to think; he really had no inclination to do so, but he forced himself.

"Now," he thought, "now that all these most transitory things have slipped away from me again, I am standing once more in the sunshine, as I once stood as a little child; nothing belongs to me; there is nothing I know how to do, nothing I am able to do, nothing that I have learned. How peculiar it is! Now, when I am no longer young, when my hair is already half gray, when my strength is giving out, now I am starting from the beginning again, from childhood!" Again he had to smile. Yes, his destiny was strange! Things were going downhill for him, and now once again he stood in the world empty, naked, and stupid. But he was unable to feel sorrow over it; no, he even felt a great urge to laugh, to laugh at himself, to laugh at this strange, foolish world.

"Things are going downhill for me!" he said to himself, laughing the while; and, as he said this, his glance fell on the river, and he saw the river going downward, too, moving constantly downstream, but singing merrily as it went. He was greatly pleased with that, and smiled at the river in a friendly way. Was this not the river in which he had wanted to drown, long ago, a hundred years ago, or had he just dreamed that?

"My life was truly peculiar," he thought; "it followed strange, roundabout paths. As a boy I was only occupied with gods and sacrifices. As a youth I was only occupied with ascetic practices, with thinking and concentrating; I was questing after *Brahman*, revering the eternal in the *Atman*. But as a young man I followed the penitents, lived in the forest, suffered from heat and cold, learned to fast, taught my body to go dead. Then, in the teachings of the great Buddha, realization came to me miraculously, I felt knowledge of the unity of the world circulating inside me like my own blood. But I had to depart even from the Buddha and the great knowledge. I went and learned the pleasures of love from Kamala, I learned business from Kamaswami, I accumulated money, I squandered money, I learned to love my belly, I learned to flatter my senses. I had to spend many years losing my intellectual powers, unlearning my ability to think, forgetting the principle of oneness. Is it not as if, slowly and wandering far from the direct path, I have changed from a man to a child, from a thinker to a child-person? And yet this journey has been very good, and yet the bird in my heart has not died. But what a journey it was! I have had to pass through so much stupidity, through so much vice, through so much error, through so much disgust and disappointment and misery, merely to become a child again and to be able to make a new start. But it all happened for the best; my heart tells me so, my eyes agree laughingly. I had to experience despair, I had to descend to the most foolish thought of all, the thought of suicide, in order to experience grace, in order to hear *om* again, to be able to sleep and awaken properly again. I had to become a fool in order to find *Atman* within myself again. I had to sin so that I could live again. Where else may my path lead me? This path is foolish, it makes wide loops, maybe it is going in a circle. Let it go wherever it wishes, I shall follow it."

He felt joy surging miraculously in his heart.

"Where," he asked his heart, "where is your jollity coming from? Is it coming from that long, good sleep that did me so much good? Or from the word *om* that I uttered? Or because I have escaped, because my getaway is accomplished, because I am finally free again and standing beneath the sky like a child? Oh, how good this escape and this liberation are! How fresh and beautiful the air is here, so good to breathe! In the place I escaped from, everything smelled of ointments, spices, wine, overabundance, indolence. How I hated that world of rich people, gourmands, gamblers! How I hated myself for remaining so long in that frightful world! How I hated myself, robbed myself, poisoned myself, tortured myself, made myself old and malevolent! No, never again will I take it into my head, as it once pleased me to do, that Siddhartha is wise! But in this I have acted well; I am glad, and I give praise for it, that that hatred for myself, that foolish, dismal life, is over and done with! I applaud you, Siddhartha; after so many years of folly, you have once again had an inspiration, you have done something, you have heard the bird in your heart singing, and you have followed it!"

Thus he applauded himself, took pleasure in himself, listened inquisitively to his stomach, which was growling with hunger. He felt that, in those last times and days, he had now thoroughly tasted and spat out a piece of sorrow, a piece of misery; he had gobbled it up to the point of despair and death. And it was good so. He might still have remained with Kamaswami for a long time, earning money, wasting money, fattening his belly and letting his soul die of thirst; he might have dwelt for a long time in that soft, well-upholstered hell, had *that* not arrived: the moment of absolute disconsolateness and despair, that extreme moment when he was suspended above the rushing waters, ready to annihilate himself. Because he had felt that despair, that most profound loathing, and had not succumbed to it; because the bird, the happy wellspring, and the voice within him were still alive after all: that is why he felt this joy, why he was laughing, why his face was beaming beneath his grayed hair.

"It is good," he thought, "to taste for yourself everything you need to know. That worldly pleasures and wealth are not good things, I learned even as a child. I knew it for a long time, but only now have I experienced it. And now I know it, I know it not only because I remember hearing it, but with my eyes, with my heart, with my stomach. And it is good for me to know it!"

He reflected for some time upon his transformation; he listened to the bird that was singing for joy. Had not that bird within him died, had he not felt its death? No, something else inside him had died, something that had long been yearning to die. Was it not the thing that he had once wanted to mortify during his ardent years as a penitent? Was it not his self, his petty, timid, proud self, with which he had battled for so many years, which had conquered him time and again, which had reemerged after every mortification, forbidding him to be happy, experiencing fear? Was it not this that had finally met its death that day, there in the forest beside that lovely river? Was it not because of that death that he was now like a child, so full of trust, so free from fear, so full of joy?

Now Siddhartha also suspected why, as a Brahman, as a penitent, he had battled in vain with that self. He had been hindered by too much knowledge, too many sacred verses, too many sacrificial rules, too much castigation, too much activity and ambition! He had been full of pride, always the cleverest, always the most eager, always one step ahead of the others, always the scholar and intellectual, always the priest or the sage. His self had wormed its way into that priesthood, into that pridefulness, into that intellectuality; there it took a firm hold and grew, while he thought he was killing it by fasting and doing penance. Now he saw it, and saw that the secret voice had been right, that no teacher would ever have been able to liberate him. For that, he had had to go into the world, he had had to lose himself to pleasure and power, to women and money; he had had to become a merchant, a dice player, a drinker, and an avaricious man, until the priest and samana within him were dead. For that, he had had to go on enduring those hateful years, enduring the disgust, the emptiness, the meaninglessness of a barren, lost life, to the very end, to the point of bitter despair, until Siddhartha the voluptuary and Siddhartha the avaricious man could also die. He *had* died; a new Siddhartha had awakened from sleep. He, too, would grow old; he, too, would have to die sometime; Siddhartha was mortal, every created thing was mortal. But today he was young, he was a child, this new Siddhartha, and he was full of joy.

These were the thoughts he was thinking as he listened smilingly to his stomach, and gratefully paid attention to the buzzing of a bee. Serenely he gazed into the flowing river; never had any water pleased him as much as this did, never had he perceived the voice and the allegory of the moving current so strongly and beautifully. He felt as if the river had something special to tell him, something he did not yet know but was still awaiting him. In this river Siddhartha had wanted to drown; in it the old, tired, despairing Siddhartha *had* drowned that day. But the new Siddhartha felt a profound love for that flowing water, and resolved in his mind not to leave it behind for quite some time.

The Ferryman

"I shall remain by this river," thought Siddhartha. "It is the same one that I once crossed on my way to the child-people; at that time a friendly ferryman took me across. I shall go to him; from his hut my path once led me to a new life, which has now grown old and has died—let my present path, too, my present new life, take its start there!"

He looked tenderly into the flowing water, into the transparent green, into the crystalline lines of its mysterious design. He saw bright pearls rising from the depths, quiet air bubbles floating on the surface, with the blue of the sky depicted in them. With a thousand eyes the river looked at him, with green ones, with white ones, with crystal ones, with sky-blue ones. How he loved that water, how it delighted him, how grateful he was to it! In his heart he heard the voice speak, the newly awakened one, and it said to him: "Love this water! Remain by it! Learn from it!" Oh, yes, he wanted to learn from it, he wanted to listen to it. Whoever understood that water and its secrets, he felt, would also understand much more, many secrets, all secrets.

But today, of all the secrets of the river, he saw just one, which gripped his soul. He saw: this water flowed and flowed, it kept on flowing, and yet it was always there; it was always and at all times the same and yet new every moment! Oh, if he could only grasp that, understand that! He did not understand or grasp it; he merely felt the stirrings of a premonition, a distant recollection, divine voices.

Siddhartha rose; the pangs of hunger in his body became unbearable. In its toils, he walked onward, up the path along the riverbank, upstream, listening to the current, listening to the growling hunger in his body.

When he reached the ferry, the boat was just in readiness, and the same ferryman who had once taken the young samana across the river was standing in the boat. Siddhartha recognized him; he, too, had greatly aged.

"Will you take me across?" he asked.

The ferryman, astonished to see such an elegant man alone and on foot, took him into the boat and shoved off.

"You have chosen a fine life," the passenger said. "It must be beautiful to live by this water every day and to travel on it."

The oarsman rocked to and fro, smiling: "It is beautiful, sir; it is just as you say. But is not every life, is not every occupation, beautiful?"

"That may be. But I envy you for yours."

"Oh, you would soon lose your pleasure in it. It is not for people in fine clothes."

Siddhartha laughed. "Earlier today I was also judged by my clothes, and was looked on with distrust. Ferryman, will you accept as a gift from me these clothes, which are a burden to me? For you ought to know, I have no money to pay you for my passage."

"You are joking, sir," the ferryman laughed.

"I am not joking, my friend. Look, once before you took me across this river in your boat, with only God repaying you. Then, do it again today, and accept my clothes in exchange."

"And do you intend to travel on without clothes, sir?"

"Oh, I would like best of all not to travel on. I would like it best of all, ferryman, if you were to give me an old apron and keep me on as your assistant—as your apprentice, rather, for I must first learn how to handle the boat."

For some time the ferryman looked at the stranger, examining him.

"Now I recognize you," he finally said. "You once slept in my hut, long ago, it must be over twenty years ago, and I took you across the river, and we said good-bye like good friends. Were you not a samana? I can no longer remember your name."

"My name is Siddhartha, and I *was* a samana when you last saw me."

"Then, welcome, Siddhartha. My name is Vasudeva. I hope you will be my guest today, too, and sleep in my hut, and tell me where you are coming from, and why your beautiful clothes are such a burden to you."

They had reached the middle of the river, and Vasudeva began to row more vigorously, to cope with the current. He worked calmly, his eyes on the bow, with powerful arms. Siddhartha sat and watched him, recalling that, even in the past, on that last day of his life as a samana, love for that man had stirred in his heart. He gratefully accepted Vasudeva's invitation. When they reached the bank, he helped him tie the boat fast to its posts; then the ferryman asked him to enter the hut, and offered him bread and water; Siddhartha ate with pleasure, and also ate with pleasure the mangos that Vasudeva offered him.

Afterward, they sat down on a tree trunk by the riverbank—it was getting on toward sunset—and Siddhartha told the ferryman about his family and his life, as he had seen it before his eyes that very day, in that hour of despair. His story lasted deep into the night.

Vasudeva listened most attentively. As he listened, he absorbed it all, family and childhood, all the learning, all the seeking, all the joy, all the distress. Among the ferryman's virtues this was one of the greatest: he knew how to listen as only few people do. Although Vasudeva said not a word, the speaker felt that he was taking in his words, quietly, openly, expectantly; that he was not losing one of them, was not awaiting them impatiently, was not assigning praise or blame to them, but was merely listening. Siddhartha realized what a great good fortune it is to confess oneself to a listener like that, to confide one's own life to his heart, one's own questing, one's own suffering.

But toward the end of Siddhartha's narrative, when he spoke about the tree by the river and his deep plunge, about the sacred *om*, and how, after his slumber, he had felt such a great love for the river, the ferryman listened with redoubled attentiveness, with total and complete devotion, his eyes closed.

But when Siddhartha ended, and a long silence had ensued, Vasudeva said: "It is just as I thought. The river spoke to you. It is a friend to you, too; it speaks to you, too. That is good, that is very good. Stay with me, Siddhartha, my friend. I once had a wife; her bed was next to mine, but she died long ago, and I have long lived alone. Now live with me, there is room and food for both."

"Thank you," said Siddhartha, "I thank you and I accept. And I also thank you, Vasudeva, for listening to me so well! It is a rare person who knows how to listen, and I have never met anyone who could do it as well as you. That is another area in which I shall learn from you."

"You will learn it," said Vasudeva, "but not from me. The river taught me how to listen, and you will learn that from it, too. It knows everything, the river, a person can learn anything from it. Look, you have already learned this, too, from the water: that it is good to make your way downward, to move lower, to seek the depths. The wealthy aristocrat Siddhartha is becoming a hired oarsman; the learned Brahman Siddhartha is becoming a ferryman: that, too, was told you by the river. You will learn the rest from it, as well."

Siddhartha said, after a long pause: "What is the rest, Vasudeva?"

Vasudeva arose. "It has grown late," he said, "let us go to bed. I cannot tell you the 'rest,' O friend. You will learn it; perhaps you already know it. Look, I am no scholar, I do not understand how to speak, nor do I understand how to think. All I know how to do is to listen, and to be pious; more than that I have never learned. If I could say it and teach it, perhaps I would be a sage, but as it is I am only a ferryman, and my task is to take people across this river. I have taken many across, thousands, and for all of them my river has meant nothing but an obstacle on their travels. They were traveling for money and on business, or to a wedding, or on a pilgrimage, and the river was in their way, and the ferryman existed only to take them past that obstacle quickly. For some among those thousands, however—just a few, four or five—the river ceased to be an obstacle; they heard its voice, they listened to it; and the river became holy for them, as it has become for me. Let us now seek repose, Siddhartha."

Siddhartha remained with the ferryman and learned how to manipulate the boat; and when there was no business at the ferry, he worked with Vasudeva in the rice paddy, gathered wood, and picked the fruit of the *pisang* trees.[11] He learned how to fashion an oar, and learned how to repair the boat, and weave baskets; and he was happy over everything he learned, and the days and months sped rapidly by. But more than Vasudeva could teach him, the river taught him. He never stopped learning from it. Above all it taught him how to listen, to listen with a quiet heart, with an open, expectant soul, without passion, without a desire, without judging, without forming an opinion.

He lived alongside Vasudeva like a friend; and at times they exchanged words with each other, words few in number but maturely considered. Vasudeva was no friend of words; Siddhartha rarely succeeded in inducing him to speak.

On one occasion, he asked him: "Have you, too, learned that secret from the river: that there is no such thing as time?"

A bright smile spread over Vasudeva's face.

---

[11] Plantain (*Musa paradisiaca*). Hesse's use of *pisang*, a Malayan word (not related to any language of India), reminds the alert reader of the true site of his so-called "Indian" sojourn.

"Yes, Siddhartha," he said. "Surely this is what you really mean: that the river is everywhere at once, at its source and at its mouth, at the waterfall, at the ferry, at the rapids, at the sea, in the mountains, everywhere, at the same time, and that it possesses only a present, without any shadow of a future?"

"That is it," said Siddhartha. "And when I had learned that, I looked at my life, and it, too, was a river, and Siddhartha the boy was separated from Siddhartha the man and from Siddhartha the old man merely by shadows, not by anything real. Moreover, Siddhartha's prior births did not constitute a past, and his death and his return to Brahma were not a future. There was nothing, there will be nothing; everything *is*, everything has substantiality and presence."

Siddhartha spoke with rapture; this enlightenment had given him profound happiness. Oh, was not all suffering time, then? Were not all self-torture and self-fearing time? Was not everything difficult, everything hostile in the world done away with and conquered as soon as you had conquered time, as soon as you could think away time? He had spoken in rapture. But Vasudeva beamed and smiled at him, nodding in confirmation; he nodded silently, stroked Siddhartha's shoulder, and turned back to his work.

And on another occasion, when the river ran high in the rainy season and roared mightily, Siddhartha said: "Is it not true, O friend, the river has many voices, very many voices? Does it not have the voice of a king, and of a warrior, and of a bull, and of a night bird, and of a woman in labor, and of a man sighing, and a thousand other voices, as well?"

"It is so," Vasudeva nodded; "the voices of all creatures are in its voice."

"And do you know," Siddhartha continued, "what word it speaks, when you succeed in hearing all its ten thousand voices at once?"

Vasudeva's face laughed happily; he leaned over to Siddhartha and pronounced the sacred *om* in his ear. And it was precisely that which Siddhartha had heard, also.

And from one occasion to another, his smile became more like the ferryman's; it became nearly as radiant, nearly as glowing with happiness, just as beaming from a thousand little wrinkles, just as childlike, just as similar to an old man's. Many travelers, seeing the two ferrymen, took them for brothers. Often, in the evening, they sat together by the riverbank on the tree trunk, in silence, both listening to the water, which was not water to them, but the voice of life, the voice of Being, of eternal Becoming. And it occurred at times that, when hearing the river, both of them thought of the same things, of a conversation they had had two days earlier, of one of their passengers whose face and destiny occupied their minds, of death, of their childhood; and, at such times, when the river had told them something good, they would look at each other simultaneously, both thinking exactly the same thing, both made happy by the identical answer to the identical question.

Something emanated from the ferry and the two ferrymen that many of their passengers perceived. It occurred at times that, after a passenger had looked into the face of one of the ferrymen, he began to recount his life; he recounted his sorrow, confessed ill deeds, sought consolation and advice. It occurred at times that one of them asked permission to spend an evening with them, in order to listen to the river. It also occurred that curiosity seekers showed up who had been told that two sages or sorcerers or saints lived at that ferry. These inquisitive people posed many questions but received no answers, and they found neither sorcerers nor sages; they found merely two friendly little old men who seemed to be mute and somewhat peculiar and simple-minded. And the inquisitive people laughed and amused themselves over the foolish and gullible way in which the common people spread such empty rumors.

The years went by, and no one counted them. Then, one day, monks came wandering by, adherents of Gotama the Buddha; they asked to be taken across the river, and from them the ferrymen learned that they were making an urgent journey back to their great teacher, because the news had spread that the Sublime One was mortally ill and would soon die his final human death,[12] in order to enter the state of salvation. Not long after that, another group of monks came by, and then another, and the monks, as well as most of the other travelers and wanderers, spoke of nothing but Gotama and his impending death. And just as, on the occasion of a military expedition or a king's coronation, people pour in from every direction and every side, and swarm like ants: in like fashion, as if drawn by a magic spell, they thronged to the place where the great Buddha awaited his death, where the tremendous event was to take place and the great Perfect One of the age was to enter into glory.

At that time Siddhartha frequently recalled the dying sage, the great teacher, whose voice had admonished nations and had awakened hundreds of thousands, whose voice he, too, had once heard, whose holy countenance he, too, had once looked upon with respect. He recalled him in a friendly way, saw his path of perfection before his eyes, and smilingly recollected the words that, as a young man, he had once

---

[12] This circumlocution corresponds to what is called in Buddhist writings the *parinirvana* of the Buddha, the "ultimate extinction" after which he would not be reborn—historically speaking, the death of Siddhartha Gautama of the Sakya clan.

addressed to him, the Sublime One. It now seemed to him that they had been prideful and precocious words; he recollected them with a smile. For some time he had known that he was no longer separated from Gotama, even though he had been unable to accept his doctrine. No, a true seeker, one who truly wished to find, could accept no doctrine. But the man who has found what he sought, such a man could approve of every doctrine, each and every one, every path, every goal; nothing separated him any longer from all those thousands of others who lived in the Eternal, who breathed the Divine.

On one of those days when so many were journeying to the dying Buddha, Kamala, too, journeyed his way, she who was formerly the most beautiful of courtesans. For some time she had retired from her previous life; she had given her garden to Gotama's monks, she had taken refuge in the Law, and was one of the friends and benefactresses of the journeying monks. Together with the boy Siddhartha, her son, upon hearing the news of Gotama's impending death, she had set out, in a simple dress, on foot. She and her young son were journeying along the river; but the boy had soon grown tired; he wanted to go back home, he wanted to rest, he wanted to eat, he became defiant and querulous. Kamala had to stop and rest with him frequently; he was accustomed to get his way where she was concerned; she had to feed him, had to console him, had to scold him. He failed to understand why he and his mother had had to undertake that laborious and sad journey to an unfamiliar place, to a man he did not know, a man who was holy and who lay dying. Let him die; what was that to the boy?

When the travelers were not far from Vasudeva's ferry, little Siddhartha once more pleaded with his mother to take a rest. She, too, Kamala, was tired out and, while the boy chewed on a plantain, she crouched down on the ground, closed her eyes a little, and rested. But suddenly she uttered a lamenting cry; the boy looked at her in alarm and saw her face pale with horror; out from under her dress escaped a little black snake, by which Kamala had been bitten.

Now they both ran hurriedly along the path, in order to reach other people, and arrived very close to the ferry, when Kamala collapsed and was unable to continue on. But the boy raised a piteous cry, from time to time kissing and hugging his mother, and she, too, added her loud calls for help to his, until the sounds reached the ears of Vasudeva, who was standing near the ferry. He ran over quickly, took the woman in his arms, and carried her into the boat; the boy ran along with them, and soon they all reached the hut, where Siddhartha was standing by the hearth engaged in lighting a fire. He looked up, and the first thing he saw was the boy's face, which strangely jogged his memory, reminding him of things forgotten. Then he saw Kamala, whom he recognized at once, although she was lying unconscious in the ferryman's arms; and then he knew that it was his own son whose face had been such a reminder to him, and his heart jumped in his bosom.

Kamala's wound was washed, but it was already black and her body had swelled; a medicinal potion was administered to her. She regained consciousness, and lay on Siddhartha's bed in the hut; and leaning over her stood Siddhartha, who had once loved her so much. It seemed like a dream to her; with a smile she looked into her friend's face; only gradually did she take in her situation, remembering the bite, and she called anxiously for the boy.

"He is here with you, do not worry," said Siddhartha.

Kamala looked into his eyes. She spoke with a heavy tongue, paralyzed by the poison. "You have grown old, dear," she said; "you have grown gray. But you look like the young samana who once came into my garden without clothes and with dusty feet. You look much more like him now than you did when you left me and Kamaswami. It is your eyes that resemble his, Siddhartha. Oh, I have grown old, too, old—did you still recognize me?"

Siddhartha smiled: "I recognized you at once, Kamala, dear."

Kamala pointed to her boy, saying: "Did you recognize him, too? He is your son."

Her eyes started to wander, and closed. The boy wept, Siddhartha took him on his knee, let him weep, stroked his hair, and, at the sight of that child's face, he recalled a Brahmanic prayer he had once learned when he himself was a little boy. Slowly, in a chanting voice, he began to say it; the words came rushing back to him from the past and his childhood. And, as he chanted, the boy grew calm, gave just a few more sobs at moments, and fell asleep. Siddhartha placed him on Vasudeva's bed. Vasudeva stood at the hearth cooking rice. Siddhartha threw him a glance that he returned with a smile.

"She is going to die," Siddhartha said softly.

Vasudeva nodded; the firelight from the hearth flickered over his friendly face.

Again Kamala regained consciousness. Her face was distorted by pain; Siddhartha's eyes read the suffering on her lips, on her pallid cheeks. He read it quietly, attentively, expectantly, absorbed in her suffering. Kamala felt it; her eyes sought his.

Looking at him, she said: "Now I see that your eyes have changed, too. They have become entirely different. What is it, then, that makes me still recognize you as being Siddhartha? You are, and you are not."

Siddhartha did not speak; silently his eyes looked into hers.

"Have you attained it?" she asked. "Have you found peace?"

He smiled and laid his hand on hers.

"I see it," she said, "I see it. I, too, shall find peace."

"You have found it," said Siddhartha in a whisper.

Kamala looked into his eyes unflinchingly. She thought about her intention to journey to Gotama to see the face of a perfected man, to absorb his peace; and she reflected that she had now found Siddhartha instead, and that it was good, just as good as if she had seen Gotama. She wanted to tell him that, but her tongue no longer obeyed her will. She looked at him in silence, and he saw life fading away in her eyes. When the final stab of pain filled her eyes and ended, when the final shudder ran through her limbs, his fingers closed her eyelids.

For a long while he sat there looking at her dead face. For a long while he contemplated her mouth, her old, tired mouth with the lips that had grown narrow, and he remembered that, once, in the springtime of his years, he had likened that mouth to a newly opened fig. For a long while he sat there, reading the pale face, the weary wrinkles; he filled himself with the sight, he saw his own face lying in the same way, just as white, just as burnt-out; and, at the same time, he saw his face and hers young, with red lips, with glowing eyes; and he was completely permeated by the feeling of present time and simultaneity, the feeling of eternity. At that moment, he felt deeply, more deeply than ever before, the indestructibility of all life, the eternity of every moment.

When he arose, Vasudeva had prepared rice for him. But Siddhartha did not eat. In the shed where they kept their goat, the two old men arranged a pallet of straw, and Vasudeva lay down to sleep. But Siddhartha went outside and sat in front of the hut all night long, listening to the river, with the past washing all around him, touched and surrounded by all the phases of his life simultaneously. But every once in a while he got up, stepped over to the door of the hut, and listened to hear whether the boy was sleeping.

Early in the morning, even before the sun became visible, Vasudeva stepped out of the shed and came over to his friend.

"You have not slept," he said.

"No, Vasudeva. I was sitting here listening to the river. It told me many things, it filled me full of healing thoughts, with the concept of oneness."

"You have experienced sorrow, Siddhartha, but I see that no sadness has entered your heart."

"No, my dear friend, why should I be sad? I, who used to be rich and happy, have now become even richer and happier. My son has been given to me."

"Let your son be welcome to me, also. But now, Siddhartha, let us go to work, there is much to be done. Kamala died on the same bed on which my wife once died. We shall also build Kamala's pyre on the same hill on which I once built my wife's pyre."

While the boy was still asleep, they built the pyre.

The Son

Timidly weeping, the boy had attended his mother's funeral; gloomy and timid, he had heard Siddhartha greet him as his son and welcome him into Vasudeva's hut. He sat pale for days on end on the dead woman's hill; he refused to eat, he averted his gaze, he locked up his heart, he resisted and fought against his destiny.

Siddhartha treated him considerately and let him have his way, out of respect for his loss. Siddhartha understood that his son did not know him, that he could not love him like a father. Gradually he also saw and understood that the eleven-year-old was a spoiled child, a mother's boy, who had grown up accustomed to riches, used to more delicate food and to a soft bed, with the habit of ordering around servants. Siddhartha understood that a spoiled child who was mourning a loss could not suddenly and voluntarily be contented with strange surroundings and poverty. He put no pressure on him, he performed many tasks for him, he always picked out the choicest pieces of food for him. He hoped he could gradually win him over through friendliness and patience.

He had considered himself rich and fortunate when the boy had come to him. But since time had gone by since then, and the boy remained a gloomy stranger, since he gave signs of having a prideful, defiant heart, refusing to do any work, showing no respect for the old men, and stealing fruit from Vasudeva's trees, Siddhartha began to understand that his son had brought him not happiness and peace but sorrow and care. But he loved him, and the sorrow and care that came with love were dearer to him than happiness and joy had been without the boy.

Ever since young Siddhartha had been in the hut, the old men had decided on a division of labor. Vasudeva had once again taken over the duties of a ferryman on his own, and Siddhartha, to be near his son, had taken over the work in the hut and the paddy.

For a long time, for long months, Siddhartha waited for his son to understand him, to accept his love, and perhaps reciprocate it. For long months Vasudeva waited, looking on, waited and kept silent. One day, when young Siddhartha had once again severely tormented his father with rebelliousness and moodiness, breaking both of his rice bowls, Vasudeva took his friend aside in the evening and spoke to him.

"Excuse me," he said, "I am talking to you like a friend. I see that you are tormenting yourself, I see that you are grieved. My dear friend, your son is giving you worries, and he is giving me worries, too. This young bird is used to a different life, a different nest. He did not, like you, run away from riches and the town out of disgust and surfeit; he had to leave all that behind against his will. I questioned the river, O friend, many times have I questioned it. But the river laughs, it laughs at me, it laughs at me and you, shaking its sides over our foolishness. Water seeks out water, the young seek out the young; your son is not in a place where he can thrive. Question the river yourself, listen to it yourself!"

Sadly Siddhartha looked into his friendly face, in the many wrinkles of which unchanging serenity dwelt.

"But can I part with him?" he asked softly, feeling ashamed. "Give me more time, dear friend! Look, I am fighting for him, I am courting his heart; I shall capture it with love and with friendly patience. Some day the river will speak to him, too; he, too, has a vocation."

Vasudeva's smile grew warmer, blossoming out. "Oh, yes, he, too, has a vocation; he, too, partakes of eternal life. But do we know, you and I, where his vocation lies, to what path, to what deeds, to what sorrows his call will lead him? His suffering will not be small, for his heart is prideful and hard; people of that sort must suffer greatly, go far astray, do much injustice, burden themselves with much sin. Tell me, dear friend: are you not bringing up your son? Do you put no pressure on him? Do you not hit him? Do you not punish him?"

"No, Vasudeva, I do none of those things."

"I knew it. You put no pressure on him, you do not hit him, you give him no orders, because you know that softness is stronger than hardness, water is stronger than rock, love is stronger than physical force. Very good, I applaud you. But is it not a mistake on your part to believe that you are not putting pressure on him or punishing him? Are you not tying him hand and foot with your love? Are you not daily shaming him, and making things even harder for him, with your kindness and patience? Are you not compelling him, proud and spoiled boy that he is, to live in a hut with two old plantain eaters, for whom even rice is a delicacy, whose thoughts cannot be his, whose hearts are old and settled and move at a different pace from his? Does not all that constitute compulsion and punishment for him?"

Taken aback, Siddhartha looked down at the ground. Quietly he asked: "What do you think I should do?"

Vasudeva said: "Take him to town, take him to his mother's house; there will still be servants there, hand him over to them. And if there are no more, take him to a teacher, not for the sake of the instruction, but so he can be among other boys, and among girls, and enter his own world. Have your never thought about that?"

"You see into my heart," said Siddhartha mournfully. "I have thought about it frequently. But look, how can I turn him over to that world, seeing that his heart is not tender to begin with? Will he not become presumptuous, will he not give himself over to pleasure and power, will he not repeat all his father's mistakes, will he not perhaps become totally lost in *samsara*?"

The ferryman flashed a bright smile; he touched Siddhartha's arm gently, saying: "Question the river about it, friend! Hear it laugh over it! Do you really believe, then, that you committed your follies in order to save your son from them? And can you protect your son against *samsara*? How? Through instruction, through prayer, through admonition? Dear friend, have you, then, completely forgotten that story, that instructive story of the Brahman's son Siddhartha that you once told me on this very spot? Who saved the samana Siddhartha from *samsara*, from sin, from avarice, from folly? Was his father's piety, were his teachers' admonitions, were his own knowledge and questing, able to save him? What father, what teacher, was able to protect him from living his own life, sullying himself with life on his own account, burdening himself with guilt on his own, drinking the bitter potion himself, finding his own path? Do you perhaps believe, dear friend, that anyone at all can be saved from that path? Your young son, perhaps, because you love him, because you would gladly spare him sorrow and pain and disappointment? But, even if you were to die for him ten times, you would not be able to abate even the tiniest part of his destiny by so doing."

Never before had Vasudeva made such a long speech.[13]

Siddhartha thanked him in a friendly way, entered the hut full of care, and was unable to sleep for some time. Vasudeva had told him nothing that he himself had not already thought and known. But it was a knowledge that he could not put into action; stronger than that knowledge was his love for the boy; his tenderness, his fear of losing him, were also stronger. For had he ever before lost his heart to anything more completely, had he ever so loved any human being, so blindly, so painfully, so unsuccessfully, and yet so happily?

Siddhartha was unable to follow his friend's advice, he was unable to give up his son. He let the boy order him around, he let the boy show disrespect for him. He remained silent and waited; daily he began all over again the unspoken battle of friendliness, the soundless war of

---

[13] It is only a few words longer than one of his speeches in the preceding chapter.

patience. Vasudeva, too, was silent and waited, friendly, knowing, forbearing. When it came to patience, they were both past masters.

On one occasion, when the boy's face reminded him strongly of Kamala, Siddhartha suddenly recalled something Kamala had once told him, long before, in his youthful days. "You cannot love," she had told him, and he had agreed with her, comparing himself to a star, and the child-people to falling leaves; and yet he had also sensed a reproach in those words. In truth, he had never been able to lose himself completely in another person, to give himself completely, to forget himself, to commit loving follies for the sake of another; he had never been able to, and, as it seemed to him at the time, that had been the great difference between him and the child-people, setting him apart. But now, ever since his son had come, now he, too, Siddhartha, had totally become a child-person, suffering for someone's sake, loving someone, lost through love, a fool for the sake of love. Now he, too, felt belatedly for once in his life that strongest and strangest of passions; he suffered from it, suffered pitifully, and yet he was blessed, and yet he was in some way renewed, in some way richer.

To be sure, he sensed that this love, this blind love for his son, was a passion, something very human, that it was *samsara*, a muddied fountain, a dark water. Nevertheless, he felt at the same time that it was not without value; it was needful, it proceeded from his own nature. This pleasure, too, had to be atoned for; these pains, too, had to be experienced; these follies, too, had to be committed.

Meanwhile his son allowed him to commit his follies, allowed him to sue for his love, allowed him to be humbled daily by his moods and caprices. There was nothing in this father that could delight him and nothing to cause him any fear. He was a good man, this father, a good, kind, gentle man, perhaps a very pious man, perhaps a saint—but none of these were qualities that could win over the boy. This father bored him, keeping him a prisoner there in his wretched hut; he bored him, and his way of responding to any misbehavior with a smile, to any insult with friendly treatment, to any malice with kindness—that was precisely the most hateful ruse of that old sneak. The boy would much have preferred for him to threaten him, beat him.

There came a day on which young Siddhartha's feelings broke out and turned openly against his father. His father had assigned him a chore, ordering him to gather brushwood. But the boy did not leave the hut; he stood there in a defiant rage, stamping his feet, clenching his fists, and, in a mighty eruption, screaming out his hatred and contempt for his father.

"Go get your own brushwood," he cried, foaming at the mouth. "I am not your servant. I know that you do not strike me, you do not dare to; I know that you are constantly trying to punish me and belittle me with your piety and your considerateness. You want me to become like you, just as pious, just as gentle, just as wise! But, listen, to spite you, I prefer to become a highway robber and murderer and go to hell, rather than become like you! I hate you, you are not my father even if you were my mother's lover ten times over!"

His anger and grief overflowed, foaming over in hostility to his father in a hundred chaotic, vicious expressions. Then the boy ran away, not returning until late in the evening.

But the following morning he had disappeared. Also gone was a little basket woven out of palm fiber of two colors, in which the ferrymen kept the copper and silver coins that they received as fare. The boat was gone, too; Siddhartha saw it lying on the far bank. The boy had run away.

"I must follow him," said Siddhartha, who had been trembling with sadness ever since the boy's insults the day before. "A child cannot walk through the forest alone. He will perish. We must build a raft, Vasudeva, to get across the river."

"We shall build a raft," said Vasudeva, "so we can recover our boat, which the boy commandeered. But as for him, you should let him go, friend; he is no longer a child, he can help himself. He is seeking the way to town, and he is right, do not forget it. He is doing what you yourself put off doing. He is watching out for himself, he is going his own way. Oh, Siddhartha, I see you suffering, but you are suffering pains that are rather laughable, that you yourself will soon laugh over."

Siddhartha made no reply. He already held the ax in his hands and was beginning to build a raft of bamboo; and Vasudeva helped him to tie the stalks together with grass ropes. Then they sailed across, were carried far downstream by the current, and pulled the raft upstream along the opposite bank.

"Why did you take along the ax?" asked Siddhartha.

Vasudeva said: "It may be that the oar of our boat is lost."

But Siddhartha knew what his friend was thinking. He was thinking that the boy would have thrown away or smashed the oar to take revenge and to hinder them in their pursuit. And indeed there was no longer an oar in the boat. Vasudeva pointed to the bottom of the boat and looked at his friend with a smile, as if to say: "Do you not see what your son is trying to tell you? Do you not see that he does not want to be followed?" But he did not say it in words. He got busy fashioning a new oar. But Siddhartha took leave of him in quest of the runaway. Vasudeva did not stop him.

When Siddhartha had already been walking through the forest for some time, the thought occurred to him that his quest was useless.

Either (as he thought) the boy was far ahead of him and already in town, or else, if he was still on the way, he would keep out of sight of his pursuer. As his thoughts evolved, he also discovered that he himself was not worried about his son, that he knew deep inside that he had neither perished nor was threatened by danger in the forest. And yet he pushed on without stopping, no longer to rescue him, but merely out of longing, merely on the chance of seeing him again. And he proceeded onward into the outskirts of town.

When he came near town on the broad highway, he stopped short, at the entrance to the beautiful pleasure garden that had once belonged to Kamala, where one day he had seen her for the first time, in the sedan chair. The past loomed up in his soul; he saw himself standing there again, young, a bearded, naked samana, his hair full of dust. For a long while Siddhartha stood looking through the open gate into the garden; he saw monks in yellow robes walking beneath the beautiful trees.

For a long while he stood there, reflecting, seeing images, listening to the story of his life. For a long while he stood there, looking at the monks, seeing instead of them the young Siddhartha, seeing the young Kamala walking beneath the tall trees. He saw himself distinctly, being entertained by Kamala, receiving her first kiss, looking back pridefully and contemptuously at his Brahman days, pridefully and longingly beginning his worldly life. He saw Kamaswami, he saw the servants, the banquets, the dice players, the musicians; he saw Kamala's songbird in its cage; he relived all this, he breathed the air of *samsara*; again he was old and tired, again he felt the disgust, again he felt the wish to obliterate himself, again he recovered, thanks to the sacred *om*.

After he had stood for some time at the garden gate, Siddhartha realized that it had been a foolish longing that had driven him to that spot, that he could not help his son, that he ought not to attach himself to him. Deeply he felt love for the runaway in his heart, like a wound, and at the same time he felt that this wound had not been given to him so that he should keep reopening it, but that it must become a blossom and emit radiance.

That at this time the wound was not yet blossoming, not yet radiant, made him sad. In place of the wishful goal that had drawn him here, in pursuit of his runaway son, there was now emptiness. Sadly he sat down; he felt something in his heart dying, he experienced emptiness, he saw no more joy, no further goal. He sat in concentration and waited. This he had learned at the river, this one thing: to wait, to be patient, to listen. And he sat and listened, in the dust of the highway; he listened to his heart beating wearily and sadly, he waited for a voice. For many an hour he crouched there, listening; he saw no more images, he was immersed in emptiness, he let himself sink into it without seeing a way out. And whenever he felt the wound smarting, he silently spoke the *om*, filled himself with *om*. The monks in the garden saw him, and, since he crouched there many hours with the dust settling on his gray hair, one of them came over and placed two *pisang* fruit on the ground in front of him. The old man did not see him.

He was awakened from that stupor by a hand touching his shoulder. Immediately he recognized that touch, gentle and shy, and came to his senses. He arose and greeted Vasudeva, who had followed him. And when he looked into Vasudeva's friendly face, into the little wrinkles that seemed to be filled with nothing but smiles, into the serene eyes, then he, too, smiled. He now saw the *pisang* fruit lying in front of him, picked them up, gave one to the ferryman, and ate the other one himself. Then he silently went back into the forest with Vasudeva, returning home to the ferry. Neither one mentioned the events of that day, neither one mentioned the boy's name, neither one mentioned his running away, neither one mentioned the wound. In the hut Siddhartha lay down on his bed, and when Vasudeva came up to him a while later to offer him a bowl of coconut milk, he found him already asleep.

Om

The wound still smarted for a long time. Siddhartha had to take across the river many a passenger who had a son or daughter with him, and not one of them did he see whom he did not envy, thinking: "So many people, so many thousands, possess this sweetest happiness—why not I? Even wicked people, even thieves and highwaymen, have children and love them, and are loved by them, only I do not." That was how uncomplicated and unreasoning his thoughts now were; that was how much like the child-people he had become.

He now looked on people differently, not as before but with less cleverness, less pride; instead, he was warmer, more curious, more concerned. When he took passengers of the ordinary sort across the river, child-people, businessmen, soldiers, womenfolk, these people did not seem so foreign to him as in the past: he understood them, he understood and shared their life, guided as it was not by ideas or insights but solely by impulses and desires; he felt he was the same as they. Although he was close to perfection and was suffering from his final wound, he nevertheless felt that these child-people were his brothers; their vanities, desires, and laughable qualities lost their laughable side for him, becoming understandable, becoming lovable, even becoming worthy of respect for him. The blind love of a mother for her child; the foolish, blind pride taken by a conceited father in his only little boy; a vain young woman's blind, wild striving for jewelry and men's admiring eyes; all these impulses, all these childish actions, all these simple, foolish, but enormously strong impulses and desires—powerfully alive, powerfully forcing their way to fruition—were now for Siddhartha no longer childish actions; he saw that people lived for their sake; for their sake he saw them accomplishing an infinity of things, traveling, waging war, suffering infinitely, enduring infinite burdens; and he was able to love them for that; he saw life, vitality, the indestructible, *Brahman*, in each of their passions, each of their deeds. These people were lovable and admirable in their blind loyalty, their blind strength and tenacity. They lacked nothing; the scholarly thinker was only superior to them in one detail, in one tiny way: he possessed the awareness, the conscious idea, of the oneness of all life. And at many times Siddhartha even doubted whether that knowledge, that idea, should be so highly valued, whether it, too, might not perhaps be a childish quality of thinking people, of the thinkers among the child-people. In every other way, worldly people were the equals of the sage, and were often far superior to him, just as animals in their dogged, relentless performance of necessary actions can at many moments appear to be superior to man.

Gradually there blossomed, gradually there ripened within Siddhartha the realization, the knowledge, of what wisdom really was, what the goal of his long quest was. It was nothing but a preparedness of the soul, a capability, a secret art of conceiving the idea of oneness at every moment, in the midst of life's activities: the ability to feel and absorb oneness. This blossomed within him slowly; he saw it reflected in Vasudeva's aged child's face: harmony, knowledge of the eternal perfection of the world, a smile, oneness.

But the wound still smarted; Siddhartha recalled his son yearningly and bitterly; he nurtured his love and tenderness in his heart; he allowed the pain to gnaw at him; he committed all the follies of love. This flame would not go out by itself.

And one day, when the wound was smarting violently, Siddhartha rowed across the river, hounded by longing; he stepped out of the boat, intending to go to town and look for his son. The river was flowing gently and quietly, it was in the dry season, but its voice had a peculiar sound: it was laughing! It was definitely laughing. The river was laughing; brightly and clearly it was laughing at the old ferryman. Siddhartha stood still, he bent over the water to hear it even better, and in the calmly moving water he saw his face reflected, and in that reflected face was something that jogged his memory, something forgotten; when he thought about it, he discovered what it was: that face resembled another that he had once known and loved and also feared. It resembled the face of his father, the Brahman. And he recollected how, long ago, as a youth, he had compelled his father to let him join the penitents, how he had taken leave of him, how he had left and never returned. Had not his father suffered the same sorrow over him that he was now suffering over his son? Had not his father died long ago, alone, without ever seeing his son again? Did not he, too, have to expect that same destiny? Was it not a comedy, a strange and stupid thing, this repetition, this running around in a disastrous circle?

The river was laughing. Yes, it was so, everything returned that had not been suffered through and untangled to the very end; the same sorrows were suffered over and over again. But Siddhartha stepped back into the boat and rowed back to the hut, recalling his father, recalling his son, laughed at by the river, at strife with himself, inclined toward despair, but no less inclined to laugh along at himself and the whole world. Ah, the wound had not yet become a blossom, his heart still resisted its fate, serenity and victory were not yet radiating from his sorrow. But he felt hope, and when he had reached the hut again, he sensed an unconquerable desire to bare his mind to Vasudeva, to show him everything, to tell all to him, that master of listening.

Vasudeva was sitting in the hut weaving a basket. He no longer went out with the ferryboat; his eyes were beginning to get weak, and not only his eyes but his arms and hands, as well. Only the joy and serene benevolence of his face were unchanged and blossoming.

Siddhartha sat down beside the old man; slowly he began to speak. He now told of things they had never discussed, his journey to town on that occasion, his smarting wound, his envy at the sight of happy fathers, his knowledge that such wishes were foolish, his futile struggle against them. He recounted everything, he was able to tell it all, even the most painful details, it became possible to say and show it all, he was able to relate it all. He openly displayed his wound, he recounted his escape of that day as well, how he had rowed across the river like a child running away, intending to walk to town, and how the river had laughed.

While he spoke, spoke for a long while, while Vasudeva listened with a calm face, Siddhartha perceived this listening of Vasudeva's more strongly than ever before; he sensed how his pains and anxieties flowed across, how his secret hope flowed across, and returned to him from the other side. To show this listener his wound was the same as bathing it in the river until it became cool and at one with the river. While he still went on speaking, still went on making admissions and making confession, Siddhartha felt more and more that it was no longer Vasudeva, no longer a human being, who was listening to him; that this motionless listener was absorbing his confession as a tree absorbs rain; that this motionless one was the river itself, God himself, the Eternal itself. And while Siddhartha ceased to think about himself and his wound, this realization of Vasudeva's altered state took possession of him; and the more he felt and penetrated this, the less strange it became and the more he saw that everything was in order and natural, that Vasudeva had been so for some time now, almost always, but that he himself had not altogether realized it; in fact, he saw that he himself was just barely different from Vasudeva. He perceived that he now saw old Vasudeva the way the common people see the gods, and that this could not last; he began to take leave of Vasudeva in his heart. And all this while he went on speaking.

When he had talked himself out, Vasudeva turned his friendly, somewhat weakened eyes toward him; he did not speak, but silently radiated love and serenity in his direction, understanding and knowledge. He took Siddhartha's hand, led him to the seat by the riverbank, sat down with him, and smiled at the river.

"You have heard it laugh," he said. "But you have not heard everything. Let us listen, you will hear more."

They listened. The many-voiced song of the river resounded gently. Siddhartha looked into the water, and in the moving water images appeared to him: his father appeared, lonely, lamenting for his son; he himself appeared, lonely, he, too, bound to his faraway son with the bonds of longing; his son appeared—he, too, the boy, lonely—raging with desire on the fiery path of his youthful wishes. Each one had his eyes on his own goal, each one was obsessed with the goal, each one was suffering. The river sang with a voice of suffering, it sang yearningly, it flowed toward its goal longingly, its voice had a lamenting sound.

"Do you hear?" asked Vasudeva's silent eyes. Siddhartha nodded.

"Listen harder!" Vasudeva whispered.

Siddhartha strove to listen harder. His father's image, his own image, his son's image, dissolved into one another; Kamala's image, too, appeared and dissolved, and Govinda's image, and other images, and overflowed into one another; they all became part of the river, as river they all pressed toward their goal, yearningly, greedily, in suffering; and the river's voice was full of longing, full of smarting pain, full of unquenchable desire. The river pressed toward its goal, Siddhartha saw it hastening, that river composed of himself and his loved ones and all the people he had ever seen; all the waves and waters hastened in their suffering toward goals, many goals, the waterfall, the lake, the rapids, the sea; and all the goals were attained, and each was followed by a new one; and the water turned into vapor and rose into the sky, it turned into rain and poured down from the sky; it turned into a fountain, into a brook, into a river; it pressed onward again, it flowed again. But the yearning voice had changed. It was still resounding, full of sorrow, searchingly, but other voices were joining it, voices of joy and sorrow, good and evil voices, laughing and mournful ones, a hundred voices, a thousand voices.

Siddhartha listened. He was now all ears, completely absorbed in his listening, completely empty, completely receptive; he felt that he had now learned all that there was to learn about listening. He had often heard all this before, these many voices in the river, but today it sounded new. By this time he could no longer distinguish the many voices, could not tell the gleeful ones from the weeping ones, the children's voices from the grown men's; they all belonged together, the lament of longing and the knowing man's laughter, the cry of anger and the moans of the dying; it was all one, it was all interwoven and knotted together, interconnected in a thousand ways. And all of this together, all the voices, all the goals, all the longing, all the suffering, all the pleasure, all the good and evil, all of this together was the world. All of this together was the river of events, the music of life. And whenever Siddhartha listened attentively to that river, that song of a thousand voices, when he listened neither to the sorrow nor the laughter, when he tied his soul not to any individual voice, entering into it with his self, but instead heard them all, perceiving the totality, the oneness, then the great song of a thousand voices consisted of a single word, which was *om*, the absolute.

"Do you hear?" Vasudeva's eyes asked again.

Vasudeva's smile beamed brightly, a glow hovered over every wrinkle in his aged face, just as the *om* hovered over all the river's voices. His smile beamed brightly as he looked at his friend, and now the same smile began to beam brightly on Siddhartha's face, too. His wound was blossoming, his sorrow was emitting rays, his self had flowed into the oneness.

In that hour Siddhartha ceased to struggle with his destiny, he ceased to suffer. On his face there blossomed the serenity of a knowledge that was no longer opposed by his will, a knowledge that knew perfection, that was in accord with the river of events, with the current of life, full of sympathy, full of shared pleasure, yielding to the current, part of the oneness.

When Vasudeva rose from the seat by the riverbank, when he looked into Siddhartha's eyes and saw the serenity of knowledge shining in them, he softly touched his shoulder with his hand, in his careful and gentle way, and said: "I have waited for this hour, dear friend. Now that it has come, let me depart. Long have I awaited this hour, long have I been the ferryman Vasudeva. Now it is enough. Farewell, hut; farewell, river; farewell, Siddhartha!"

Siddhartha made a low bow to the departing one.

"I knew it," he said quietly. "Will you go into the forests?"

"I go into the forests, I go into oneness," said Vasudeva radiantly.

Radiantly he made his departure; Siddhartha watched him go. With profound joy, with profound gravity, he watched him go, seeing his steps full of peace, seeing his head full of brightness, seeing his figure full of light.

Govinda

On one occasion, during a period of rest, Govinda was dwelling with other monks in the pleasure grove that the courtesan Kamala had given to Gotama's disciples. He heard reports about an old ferryman who lived a day's journey away by the river and whom many people regarded as a sage. When Govinda continued his journey, he chose the path to the ferry, desirous of seeing that ferryman. For, even though he had lived by the Buddhist rules all his life and was looked on with respect by the younger monks because of his age and his modesty, nevertheless the restlessness and seeking had never been extinguished in his heart.

He came to the river, he asked the old man to take him across, and when they were getting out of the boat on the other side, he said to the old man: "You are a great benefactor to us monks and pilgrims, you have already taken many of us across the river. Are not you, too, ferryman, one who seeks after the true path?"

Siddhartha said, with a smile in his old eyes: "Do you call yourself one who seeks, O venerable one, although you are already well advanced in years and you wear the robe of Gotama's monks?"

"To be sure, I am old," said Govinda, "but I have never ceased to seek. I shall never cease to seek; that seems to be my destiny. You, too, I believe, have sought. Will you tell me anything about it, honored sir?"

Siddhartha said: "What could I possibly have to tell you, venerable one? Perhaps that you are doing too much seeking? That your seeking prevents you from finding?"

"How is that?" Govinda asked.

"When someone seeks," Siddhartha said, "it is all too easy for his eyes to see nothing but the thing he seeks, so that he is unable to find anything or absorb anything because he is always thinking exclusively about what he seeks, because he has a goal, because he is obsessed by that goal. Seeking means having a goal. But finding means being free, remaining accessible, having no goal. You, venerable one, are perhaps really one who seeks, because, pressing after your goal, you fail to see many a thing that is right before your eyes."

"I still do not understand completely," said Govinda, and asked: "How do you mean that?"

Siddhartha said: "Once before, O venerable one, many years ago, you were at this river, and by the river you found a man asleep and sat down near him to guard him while he slept. But, O Govinda, you did not recognize the sleeper."

Astonished, like a man under a spell, the monk looked into the ferryman's eyes.

"Are you Siddhartha?" he asked timidly. "I would not have recognized you this time, either! I greet you warmly, Siddhartha; I am sincerely glad to see you again. You have changed a great deal, friend. — And so you have now become a ferryman?"

Siddhartha gave a friendly laugh. "A ferryman, yes. Govinda, many people must change a great deal and must wear all sorts of garments; I am one of those, my dear friend. Welcome, Govinda, please spend the night in my hut."

Govinda spent the night in the hut, sleeping on the bed that had once been Vasudeva's bed. He asked many questions of the friend of his youth; Siddhartha had to tell him many events of his life.

On the following morning, when it was time to set out on his day's journey, Govinda said, not without hesitation: "Before I continue my travels, Siddhartha, permit me one more question. Do you have a doctrine? Do you have a faith or a body of knowledge that you follow, that helps you live and act properly?"

Siddhartha said: "You know, my dear friend, that even as a young man, at the time when we were living with the penitents in the forest, I arrived at the point of distrusting teachings and teachers, and of turning my back on them. I have retained that attitude. And yet, since then I have had many teachers. For a long time a beautiful courtesan was my teacher, and a wealthy merchant was my teacher, and a few dice players. Once, a wandering disciple of the Buddha was also my teacher; he sat with me when I had fallen asleep in the forest, in the course of wandering. I learned from him, too; I am grateful to him, too, very grateful. But I have learned the most here, from this river and from my predecessor, the ferryman Vasudeva. He was a very simple man, was Vasudeva; he was no thinker, but he knew what was necessary as well as Gotama did; he was a perfected man, a saint."

Govinda said: "O Siddhartha, it seems to me you still enjoy making a little fun of people. I believe you and I know that you did not follow any particular teacher. But have you not yourself found, even if not a doctrine, then at least certain ideas, certain realizations, that are your own and help you to live? If you wished to tell me anything about them, you would gladden my heart."

Siddhartha said: "Yes, I have had ideas and realizations, from time to time. On occasions, for an hour or for a day, I have felt knowledge in myself, just as a man feels life in his heart. Those thoughts were numerous, but it would be hard for me to communicate them to you. Look, my dear Govinda, here is one of the thoughts I discovered: Wisdom cannot be imparted. Wisdom that a wise man attempts to impart always sounds like foolishness."

"Are you joking?" Govinda asked.

"I am not joking. I am telling you what I discovered. Knowledge can be imparted, but not wisdom. You can discover it, it can guide your life, it can bear you up, you can do miracles with it, but you cannot tell it or teach it. This was what I had several premonitions of, even as a youngster; it was this that drove me away from teachers. I have discovered an idea, Govinda, which you will once again consider to be a joke or foolishness, but which is my best idea. Namely: the opposite of every truth is equally true! What I mean is: without fail, a truth can only be uttered and clothed in words if it is one-sided. Everything is one-sided if the mind can conceive it and words can express it; all of that is one-sided, all of that is a half-truth, all of that lacks completeness, roundedness, oneness. Whenever the sublime Gotama spoke about the world in his sermons, he had to divide it into *samsara* and *nirvana*, into illusion and truth, into suffering and salvation. You have no alternative, there is no other method for a man who wants to teach. But the world itself, what exists around us and inside us, is never one-sided. A person or an action is never totally *samsara* or totally *nirvana*; a person is never totally saintly or totally sinful. Because we are subject to illusion, it does actually look as if time were something real. Time is not real, Govinda; I have learned that over and over again. And, if time is not real, the span that seems to exist between world and eternity, between sorrow and bliss, between evil and good, is also an illusion."

"How so?" Govinda asked nervously.

"Pay close attention, dear friend, pay close attention! A sinner, such as you and I are, is a sinner, but some day he will be Brahma again, some day he will attain *nirvana*, he will be a Buddha—and now see: that 'some day' is an illusion, it is only a metaphor! The sinner is not journeying toward Buddhahood, he is not caught up in an evolution, even though our thought processes are unable to imagine things differently. No, the sinner contains the future Buddha, now and today he already is that Buddha; his future is already completely there; you must revere the becoming, the possible, the concealed Buddha in him, in yourself, in everyone. The world, friend Govinda, is not imperfect or on a slow journey toward perfection; no, it is perfect at every moment; all sin already bears its forgiveness within itself; every little boy already bears the old man within himself, every infant bears death, every dying man bears eternal life. No one is able to look at someone else and know how far along on his journey he is; in the highwayman and dice player lurks a Buddha, in the Brahman lurks the highwayman. In profound meditation there is the possibility of abolishing time, of seeing all past, present, and future life as being simultaneous; and there everything is good, everything is perfect, everything is *Brahman*. Therefore, whatever exists seems good to me; death is like life to me, sin like sanctity, cleverness like folly; everything must be as it is; everything needs only my consent, my willingness, my loving comprehension, and then it is good in my eyes, and can never harm me. I learned from my body and my soul that I was in great need of sin; I needed sensual pleasures, the ambition for possessions, vanity, and I needed the most humiliating despair in order to learn how to give up my resistance, in order to learn how to love the world, in order to cease comparing it with some world of my wishes or my imagination, with some type of perfection that I had concocted, but to leave it the way it is, to love it, and to be a part of it gladly. — These, O Govinda, are a few of the ideas that have come into my mind."

Siddhartha stooped down, picked up a stone from the ground, and weighed it in his hand.

"This," he said effortlessly, as if at play, "is a stone, and within a certain time it will perhaps be earth, and from earth it will become a plant or an animal or a person. Now, in the past I would have said: 'This stone is merely a stone, it is worthless, it belongs to the world of *maya*; but, because in the cycle of transformations it may also become a person and an intellect, I assign some value even to it.' That is how I might once have reasoned. But today I think: this stone is a stone, it is also an animal, it is also a god, it is also Buddha; I do not revere and love it because it may some day become one thing or another, but because it has for a long time, always, been everything — and it is precisely the fact of its being a stone, of its appearing to me as a stone now and today, that makes me love it and see value and meaning in each of its veins and cavities, in the yellow, in the gray, in its hardness, in the ring it emits when I strike it, in the dryness or moistness of its surface. There are stones that feel like oil or soap to the touch, and others like leaves, others like sand; and each one is special and prays '*om*' in its own way, each one is *Brahman*; but, at the same time and just as much, it is a stone, it is oily or soapy; and that is precisely what I like and find marvelous and worthy of adoration. — But do not let me say any more about this. Words do no good to the secret meaning; everything always immediately becomes a little different when you express it, a little falsified, a little foolish—yes, and that, too, is very good and pleases me greatly, I am also perfectly contented that one person's treasure of wisdom always sounds like foolishness to someone else."

Govinda listened in silence.

"Why did you tell me that about the stone?" he asked hesitantly after a pause.

"I did it unintentionally. Or perhaps it was intended to show that I love the stone, and the river, and all these things we look at and can learn from. I can love a stone, Govinda, and also a tree or a piece of bark. They are physical things, and things can be loved. But words I cannot love. Therefore, teachings mean nothing to me; they possess neither hardness, nor softness, nor colors, nor edges, nor odor, nor taste; they possess nothing but words. Perhaps that is what prevents you from finding peace, perhaps it is all those words. For even salvation and virtue, even *samsara* and *nirvana*, are mere words, Govinda. There is no thing that is *nirvana*, there is only the word *nirvana*."

Govinda said: "My friend, *nirvana* is not merely a word; it is a concept."

Siddhartha continued: "A concept, maybe so. I must confess to you, dear friend: I do not make a great distinction between concepts and words. To put it frankly, I have no high regard for concepts, either. I have a higher regard for physical things. Here on this ferryboat, for example, a man was my predecessor and teacher, a saintly man; for many years he simply believed in the river, and nothing else. He observed that the river's voice spoke to him; he learned from that voice, it educated and instructed him; the river was like a god to him; for many years he did not know that every wind, every cloud, every bird, every beetle, is just as godlike, knows just as much and can teach as much as the river he venerated. But when that saintly man left for the forests, he knew everything, he knew more than you and I, without teachers, without books, merely because he had believed in the river."

Govinda said: "But is that which you call 'physical things' something real, something substantial? Is that not merely a ruse of *maya*, merely an image and an illusion? Your stone, your tree, your river—are they realities?"

Siddhartha said: "That does not trouble me very much, either. The things may be illusory or not; if they are, I, too, am illusory, and so they continue to be of the same nature as myself. That is what makes them so dear and worthy of reverence to me: they share my nature. Therefore I can love them. And this now is a doctrine that you will laugh at: love, O Govinda, appears to me to be the chief thing of all. To penetrate the world's secrets, to explain its workings, and to despise it, may be the proper occupation of great thinkers. But my sole concern is to be able to love the world, not to despise it, not to hate it or myself, to be able to look at it and myself and all beings with love and admiration and respect."

"I understand that," said Govinda. "But it was just this that he, the Sublime One, recognized as illusion. He requires of us benevolence, considerateness, sympathy, forbearance, but not love; he forbade us to tie our hearts in love to earthly things."

"I know," said Siddhartha; his smile was like golden beams. "I know, Govinda. And behold, here we are amid the jungle of opinions, quarreling over words. For I cannot deny it, my words about love contradict, or apparently contradict, Gotama's words. For that very reason I distrust words so much, for I know that that contradiction is illusory. I know that I agree with Gotama. How, then, could he, of all people, fail to be acquainted with love? He, who recognized the transitoriness and nothingness of all human existence, and yet loved people so much that he spent a long, laborious life doing nothing but helping them, teaching them! Even in his case, even in the case of your great teacher, the fact is dearer to me than words, his activities and life more important than his sermons, the gesture of his hands more important than his opinions. I see his greatness not in his sermons or his thoughts, but only in his activities, in his life."

For a long while the two old men were silent. Then Govinda said, as he bowed in farewell: "Thank you, Siddhartha, for telling me some of your ideas. They are partly strange ideas; I was not able to understand all of them immediately. Be that as it may, I thank you and I wish you peaceful days."

(But secretly he thought to himself: "This Siddhartha is a peculiar person, he expresses peculiar ideas, his doctrine sounds foolish. Not so the pure doctrine of the Sublime One, which is clearer, purer, more comprehensible, and which contains nothing strange, foolish, or laughable. But Siddhartha's ideas seem to me to be unlike his hands and feet, his eyes, his forehead, his breathing, his smile, his greeting, his way of walking. Never, since our sublime Gotama entered *nirvana*, never since then have I come across a person about whom I felt: this is a saint! Him alone, this Siddhartha, have I found to be so. Even if his doctrine is strange, even if his words sound foolish, nevertheless his eyes and his hands, his skin and his hair, everything about him radiates a purity, radiates a peace, radiates a serenity and mildness and sanctity that I have not seen in any other person since the final death of our sublime teacher.") While Govinda was thinking this and there was a contradiction in his heart, he bowed to Siddhartha again, attracted by love. He made a low bow to the one who sat there calmly.

"Siddhartha," he said, "we have become old men. We shall hardly meet again in our present forms. I see, beloved friend, that you have found peace. I confess that I have not. Tell me, honored one, one thing more; let me take away with me something that I can grasp, that I can understand! Give me something to accompany me on my path. My path is often wearisome, often gloomy, Siddhartha."

Siddhartha, remaining silent, looked at him with that unchanging, quiet smile. Govinda stared into his face, with anguish, with longing. Sorrow and eternal seeking were written in his gaze, eternal inability to find what he sought.

Siddhartha saw it and smiled.

"Lean over to me!" he whispered softly in Govinda's ear. "Lean over here to me! Like that, even closer! Very close! Kiss me on the forehead, Govinda!"

But while Govinda, amazed but impelled by great love and presentiment, obeyed his words, leaned over close to him, and touched his forehead with his lips, something miraculous happened to him. While his thoughts still lingered over Siddhartha's peculiar words, while he was still futilely and reluctantly struggling to think away time and imagine *nirvana* and *samsara* as one and the same thing, while a certain contempt for his friend's words was even fighting within him against a tremendous love and respect, this is what happened to him:

He no longer saw his friend Siddhartha's face; in its place he saw other faces, many of them, a long series, a flowing river of faces, hundreds, thousands, all of them arising and dissolving, and yet all seeming to be there at the same time; they all constantly changed and renewed themselves, and yet were all Siddhartha. He saw the face of a fish, a carp, its mouth opened in infinite pain, a dying fish with eyes glazing over—he saw the face of a newborn child, red and full of wrinkles, distorted in weeping—he saw the face of a murderer, saw him plunge a knife into someone's body—in the same second he saw that criminal bound and kneeling and his head being cut off by the executioner with the stroke of a sword—he saw the bodies of men and women naked in the positions and battles of furious love—he saw corpses stretched out, quiet, cold, empty—he saw heads of animals, of boars, of crocodiles, of elephants, of bulls, of birds—he saw gods, saw Krishna, saw Agni—he saw all these forms and faces interrelating in a thousand ways, each form helping the other, loving it, hating it, annihilating it, giving birth to it again; each one was a death wish, a passionately painful confession of mortality; and yet none of them died, each one was merely transformed, was constantly reborn, constantly received a new face, but without any time elapsing between one face and the next—and all these forms and faces were in repose, flowed, engendered themselves, drifted away and poured into one another; and all of them were constantly covered by something thin, insubstantial, yet existent, like a thin layer of glass or ice, like a transparent skin, a shell or mold or mask of water; and this mask smiled, and this mask was Siddhartha's smiling face, which he, Govinda, was touching with his lips at that very moment. And Govinda saw that this smile on the mask, this smile of oneness over the flowing shapes, this smile of simultaneity over the thousand births and deaths, this smile of Siddhartha's, was exactly the same, was exactly the same quiet, subtle, impenetrable, perhaps kindly, perhaps mocking, wise, thousandfold smile of Gotama, the Buddha, which he had seen with respect a hundred times. Thus, Govinda knew, do the perfect ones smile.

No longer knowing whether time existed, whether that vision had lasted a second or a hundred years; no longer knowing whether a Siddhartha, a Gotama, an "I" or a "you" existed; wounded in his inmost recesses as if by a divine arrow, the wound from which tastes sweet; enchanted and dissolved in his inmost being, Govinda stood there a little while longer, leaning over Siddhartha's quiet face, which he had just kissed, which had just been the theater of all formations, of all becoming, of all being. The countenance was unchanged, now that the depths of multiplicity beneath its surface had been shut away again; it was quietly smiling, softly and gently smiling, perhaps in a very kindly way, perhaps in a very mocking way, exactly as *he* had smiled, the Sublime One.

Govinda made a low bow; tears, of which he knew nothing, ran down his aged face; the sensation of the warmest love, of the most humble veneration, burned like a fire in his heart. He made a low bow, down to the ground, before the man sitting motionless there, whose smile reminded him of everything he had ever loved in his life, everything that had ever been valuable and sacred to him in his life.

DOVER · THRIFT · EDITIONS

POETRY

"MINIVER CHEEVY" AND OTHER POEMS, Edwin Arlington Robinson. 64pp. 28756-4 $1.00

EARLY POEMS, Ezra Pound. 80pp. (Available in U.S. only) 28745-9 $1.00

EARLY POEMS, William Carlos Williams. 64pp. (Available in U.S. only) 29294-0 $1.00

"THE WASTE LAND" AND OTHER POEMS, T. S. Eliot. 64pp. (Available in U.S. only) 40061-1 $1.00

RENASCENCE AND OTHER POEMS, Edna St. Vincent Millay. 64pp. (Available in U.S. only) 26873-X $1.00

SELECTED POEMS, John Milton. 128pp. 27554-X $1.50

SELECTED CANTERBURY TALES, Geoffrey Chaucer. 144pp. 28241-4 $1.00

GREAT SONNETS, Paul Negri (ed.). 96pp. 28052-7 $1.00

CIVIL WAR POETRY: An Anthology, Paul Negri. 128pp. 29883-3 $1.50

WAR IS KIND AND OTHER POEMS, Stephen Crane. 64pp. 40424-2 $1.00

THE RAVEN AND OTHER FAVORITE POEMS, Edgar Allan Poe. 64pp. 26685-0 $1.00

ESSAY ON MAN AND OTHER POEMS, Alexander Pope. 128pp. 28053-5 $1.50

GOBLIN MARKET AND OTHER POEMS, Christina Rossetti. 64pp. 28055-1 $1.00

CHICAGO POEMS, Carl Sandburg. 80pp. 28057-8 $1.00

THE SHOOTING OF DAN MCGREW AND OTHER POEMS, Robert Service. 96pp. (Available in U.S. only) 27556-6 $1.00

COMPLETE SONNETS, William Shakespeare. 80pp. 26686-9 $1.00

SELECTED POEMS, Percy Bysshe Shelley. 128pp. 27558-2 $1.50

100 BEST-LOVED POEMS, Philip Smith (ed.). 96pp. 28553-7 $1.00

101 GREAT AMERICAN POEMS, The American Poetry & Literacy Project (ed.). (Available in U.S. only) 40158-8 $1.00

NATIVE AMERICAN SONGS AND POEMS: An Anthology, Brian Swann (ed.). 64pp. 29450-1 $1.00

SELECTED POEMS, Alfred Lord Tennyson. 112pp. 27282-6 $1.00

LITTLE ORPHANT ANNIE AND OTHER POEMS, James Whitcomb Riley. 80pp. 28260-0 $1.00

CHRISTMAS CAROLS: COMPLETE VERSES, Shane Weller (ed.). 64pp. 27397-0 $1.00

GREAT LOVE POEMS, Shane Weller (ed.). 128pp. 27284-2 $1.00

LOVE: A Book of Quotations, Herb Galewitz (ed.). 64pp. 40004-2 $1.00

EVANGELINE AND OTHER POEMS, Henry Wadsworth Longfellow. 64pp. 28255-4 $1.00

CIVIL WAR POETRY AND PROSE, Walt Whitman. 96pp. 28507-3 $1.00

SELECTED POEMS, Walt Whitman. 128pp. 26878-0 $1.00

THE BALLAD OF READING GAOL AND OTHER POEMS, Oscar Wilde. 64pp. 27072-6 $1.00

FAVORITE POEMS, William Wordsworth. 80pp. 27073-4 $1.00

WORLD WAR ONE BRITISH POETS: Brooke, Owen, Sassoon, Rosenberg and Others, Candace Ward (ed.). (Available in U.S. only) 29568-0 $1.00

THE CAVALIER POETS: An Anthology, Thomas Crofts (ed.). 80pp. 28766-1 $1.00

ENGLISH ROMANTIC POETRY: An Anthology, Stanley Appelbaum (ed.). 256pp. 29282-7 $2.00

EARLY POEMS, William Butler Yeats. 128pp. 27808-5 $1.50

"EASTER, 1916" AND OTHER POEMS, William Butler Yeats. 80pp. (Available in U.S. only) 29771-3 $1.00

DOVER · THRIFT · EDITIONS

FICTION

FLATLAND: A ROMANCE OF MANY DIMENSIONS, Edwin A. Abbott. 96pp. 27263-X $1.00

PERSUASION, Jane Austen. 224pp. 29555-9 $2.00

PRIDE AND PREJUDICE, Jane Austen. 272pp. 28473-5 $2.00

SENSE AND SENSIBILITY, Jane Austen. 272pp. 29049-2 $2.00

WUTHERING HEIGHTS, Emily Brontë. 256pp. 29256-8 $2.00

BEOWULF, Beowulf (trans. by R. K. Gordon). 64pp. 27264-8 $1.00

CIVIL WAR STORIES, Ambrose Bierce. 128pp. 28038-1 $1.00

THE AUTOBIOGRAPHY OF AN EX-COLORED MAN, James Weldon Johnson. 112pp. 28512-X $1.00

TARZAN OF THE APES, Edgar Rice Burroughs. 224pp. (Available in U.S. only) 29570-2 $2.00

ALICE'S ADVENTURES IN WONDERLAND, Lewis Carroll. 96pp. 27543-4 $1.00

O PIONEERS!, Willa Cather. 128pp. 27785-2 $1.00

MY ÁNTONIA, Willa Cather. 176pp. 28240-6 $2.00

PAUL'S CASE AND OTHER STORIES, Willa Cather. 64pp. 29057-3 $1.00

IN A GERMAN PENSION: 13 Stories, Katherine Mansfield. 112pp. 28719-X $1.50

THE STORY OF AN AFRICAN FARM, Olive Schreiner. 256pp. 40165-0 $2.00

"THE YELLOW WALLPAPER" AND OTHER STORIES, Charlotte Perkins Gilman. 80pp. 29857-4 $1.00

HERLAND, Charlotte Perkins Gilman. 128pp. 40429-3 $1.50

FIVE GREAT SHORT STORIES, Anton Chekhov. 96pp. 26463-7 $1.00

"THE FIDDLER OF THE REELS" AND OTHER SHORT STORIES, Thomas Hardy. 80pp. 29960-0 $1.50

FAVORITE FATHER BROWN STORIES, G. K. Chesterton. 96pp. 27545-0 $1.00

THE WARDEN, Anthony Trollope. 176pp. 40076-X $2.00

THE COUNTRY OF THE POINTED FIRS, Sarah Orne Jewett. 96pp. 28196-5 $1.00

GREAT SHORT STORIES BY AMERICAN WOMEN, Candace Ward (ed.). 192pp. 28776-9 $2.00

SHORT STORIES, Louisa May Alcott. 64pp. 29063-8 $1.00

THE AWAKENING, Kate Chopin. 128pp. 27786-0 $1.00

A PAIR OF SILK STOCKINGS AND OTHER STORIES, Kate Chopin. 64pp. 29264-9 $1.00

THE REVOLT OF "MOTHER" AND OTHER STORIES, Mary E. Wilkins Freeman. 128pp. 40428-5 $1.50

HEART OF DARKNESS, Joseph Conrad. 80pp. 26464-5 $1.00

THE SECRET SHARER AND OTHER STORIES, Joseph Conrad. 128pp. 27546-9 $1.00

THE "LITTLE REGIMENT" AND OTHER CIVIL WAR STORIES, Stephen Crane. 80pp. 29557-5 $1.00

THE OPEN BOAT AND OTHER STORIES, Stephen Crane. 128pp. 27547-7 $1.50

THE RED BADGE OF COURAGE, Stephen Crane. 112pp. 26465-3 $1.00

A CHRISTMAS CAROL, Charles Dickens. 80pp. 26865-9 $1.00

THE CRICKET ON THE HEARTH AND OTHER CHRISTMAS STORIES, Charles Dickens. 128pp. 28039-X $1.00

THE DOUBLE, Fyodor Dostoyevsky. 128pp. 29572-9 $1.50

NOTES FROM THE UNDERGROUND, Fyodor Dostoyevsky. 96pp. 27053-X $1.00

THE GAMBLER, Fyodor Dostoyevsky. 112pp. 29081-6 $1.50

THE ADVENTURE OF THE DANCING MEN AND OTHER STORIES, Sir Arthur Conan Doyle. 80pp. 29558-3 $1.00

THE HOUND OF THE BASKERVILLES, Arthur Conan Doyle. 128pp. 28214-7 $1.00

SIX GREAT SHERLOCK HOLMES STORIES, Sir Arthur Conan Doyle. 112pp. 27055-6 $1.00

SILAS MARNER, George Eliot. 160pp. 29246-0 $1.50

FICTION

MADAME BOVARY, Gustave Flaubert. 256pp. 29257-6 $2.00

WHERE ANGELS FEAR TO TREAD, E. M. Forster. 128pp. (Available in U.S. only) 27791-7 $1.50

A ROOM WITH A VIEW, E. M. Forster. 176pp. (Available in U.S. only) 28467-0 $2.00

THE OVERCOAT AND OTHER STORIES, Nikolai Gogol. 112pp. 27057-2 $1.50

GREAT GHOST STORIES, John Grafton (ed.). 112pp. 27270-2 $1.00

"THE MOONLIT ROAD" AND OTHER GHOST AND HORROR STORIES, Ambrose Bierce (John Grafton, ed.) 96pp. 40056-5 $1.00

THE MABINOGION, Lady Charlotte E. Guest. 192pp. 29541-9 $2.00

WINESBURG, OHIO, Sherwood Anderson. 160pp. 28269-4 $2.00

THE LUCK OF ROARING CAMP AND OTHER STORIES, Bret Harte. 96pp. 27271-0 $1.00

THIS SIDE OF PARADISE, F. Scott Fitzgerald. 208pp. 28999-0 $2.00

"THE DIAMOND AS BIG AS THE RITZ" AND OTHER STORIES, F. Scott Fitzgerald. 29991-0 $2.00

THE SCARLET LETTER, Nathaniel Hawthorne. 192pp. 28048-9 $2.00

YOUNG GOODMAN BROWN AND OTHER STORIES, Nathaniel Hawthorne. 128pp. 27060-2 $1.00

THE GIFT OF THE MAGI AND OTHER SHORT STORIES, O. Henry. 96pp. 27061-0 $1.00

THE NUTCRACKER AND THE GOLDEN POT, E. T. A. Hoffmann. 128pp. 27806-9 $1.00

THE BEAST IN THE JUNGLE AND OTHER STORIES, Henry James. 128pp. 27552-3 $1.00

DAISY MILLER, Henry James. 64pp. 28773-4 $1.00

WASHINGTON SQUARE, Henry James. 176pp. 40431-5 $2.00

THE TURN OF THE SCREW, Henry James. 96pp. 26684-2 $1.00

DUBLINERS, James Joyce. 160pp. 26870-5 $1.00

A PORTRAIT OF THE ARTIST AS A YOUNG MAN, James Joyce. 192pp. 28050-0 $2.00

DEATH IN VENICE, Thomas Mann. 96pp. (Available in U.S. only) 28714-9 $1.00

THE METAMORPHOSIS AND OTHER STORIES, Franz Kafka. 96pp. 29030-1 $1.50

THE MAN WHO WOULD BE KING AND OTHER STORIES, Rudyard Kipling. 128pp. 28051-9 $1.50

SREDNI VASHTAR AND OTHER STORIES, Saki (H. H. Munro). 96pp. 28521-9 $1.00

THE OIL JAR AND OTHER STORIES, Luigi Pirandello. 96pp. 28459-X $1.00

SELECTED SHORT STORIES, D. H. Lawrence. 128pp. 27794-1 $1.00

GREEN TEA AND OTHER GHOST STORIES, J. Sheridan LeFanu. 96pp. 27795-X $1.00

SHORT STORIES, Theodore Dreiser. 112pp. 28215-5 $1.50

THE CALL OF THE WILD, Jack London. 64pp. 26472-6 $1.00

FIVE GREAT SHORT STORIES, Jack London. 96pp. 27063-7 $1.00

WHITE FANG, Jack London. 160pp. 26968-X $1.00

THE NECKLACE AND OTHER SHORT STORIES, Guy de Maupassant. 128pp. 27064-5 $1.00

BARTLEBY AND BENITO CERENO, Herman Melville. 112pp. 26473-4 $1.00

THE GOLD-BUG AND OTHER TALES, Edgar Allan Poe. 128pp. 26875-6 $1.00

TALES OF TERROR AND DETECTION, Edgar Allan Poe. 96pp. 28744-0 $1.00

DETECTION BY GASLIGHT, Douglas G. Greene (ed.). 272pp. 29928-7 $2.00

THE THIRTY-NINE STEPS, John Buchan. 96pp. 28201-5 $1.50

THE QUEEN OF SPADES AND OTHER STORIES, Alexander Pushkin. 128pp. 28054-3 $1.50

FIRST LOVE AND DIARY OF A SUPERFLUOUS MAN, Ivan Turgenev. 96pp. 28775-0 $1.50

FATHERS AND SONS, Ivan Turgenev. 176pp. 40073-5 $2.00

FRANKENSTEIN, Mary Shelley. 176pp. 28211-2 $1.00

THREE LIVES, Gertrude Stein. 176pp. (Available in U.S. only) 28059-4 $2.00

FICTION

THE STRANGE CASE OF DR. JEKYLL AND MR. HYDE, Robert Louis Stevenson. 64pp. 26688-5 $1.00

TREASURE ISLAND, Robert Louis Stevenson. 160pp. 27559-0 $1.50

THE LOST WORLD, Arthur Conan Doyle. 176pp. 40060-3 $1.50

GULLIVER'S TRAVELS, Jonathan Swift. 240pp. 29273-8 $2.00

ROBINSON CRUSOE, Daniel Defoe. 288pp. 40427-7 $2.00

THE KREUTZER SONATA AND OTHER SHORT STORIES, Leo Tolstoy. 144pp. 27805-0 $1.50

THE IMMORALIST, André Gide. 112pp. (Available in U.S. only) 29237-1 $1.50

ADVENTURES OF HUCKLEBERRY FINN, Mark Twain. 224pp. 28061-6 $2.00

THE ADVENTURES OF TOM SAWYER, Mark Twain. 192pp. 40077-8 $2.00

THE MYSTERIOUS STRANGER AND OTHER STORIES, Mark Twain. 128pp. 27069-6 $1.00

HUMOROUS STORIES AND SKETCHES, Mark Twain. 80pp. 29279-7 $1.00

YOU KNOW ME AL, Ring Lardner. 128pp. 28513-8 $1.00

MOLL FLANDERS, Daniel Defoe. 256pp. 29093-X $2.00

CANDIDE, Voltaire (François-Marie Arouet). 112pp. 26689-3 $1.00

"THE COUNTRY OF THE BLIND" AND OTHER SCIENCE-FICTION STORIES, H. G. Wells. 160pp. (Available in U.S. only) 29569-9 $1.00

THE ISLAND OF DR. MOREAU, H. G. Wells. (Available in U.S. only) 29027-1 $1.00

THE INVISIBLE MAN, H. G. Wells. 112pp. (Available in U.S. only) 27071-8 $1.00

THE TIME MACHINE, H. G. Wells. 80pp. (Available in U.S. only) 28472-7 $1.00

LOOKING BACKWARD, Edward Bellamy. 160pp. 29038-7 $2.00

THE WAR OF THE WORLDS, H. G. Wells. 160pp. (Available in U.S. only) 29506-0 $1.00

ETHAN FROME, Edith Wharton. 96pp. 26690-7 $1.00

SHORT STORIES, Edith Wharton. 128pp. 28235-X $1.00

THE AGE OF INNOCENCE, Edith Wharton. 288pp. 29803-5 $2.00

THE MOON AND SIXPENCE, W. Somerset Maugham. 176pp. (Available in U.S. only) 28731-9 $2.00

THE PICTURE OF DORIAN GRAY, Oscar Wilde. 192pp. 27807-7 $1.50

MONDAY OR TUESDAY: Eight Stories, Virginia Woolf. 64pp. (Available in U.S. only) 29453-6 $1.00

JACOB'S ROOM, Virginia Woolf. 144pp. (Available in U.S. only) 40109-X $1.50

NONFICTION

THE DEVIL'S DICTIONARY, Ambrose Bierce. 144pp. 27542-6 $1.00

DE PROFUNDIS, Oscar Wilde. 64pp. 29308-4 $1.00

OSCAR WILDE'S WIT AND WISDOM: A Book of Quotations, Oscar Wilde. 64pp. 40146-4 $1.00

THE SOULS OF BLACK FOLK, W. E. B. Du Bois. 176pp. 28041-1 $2.00

NARRATIVE OF THE LIFE OF FREDERICK DOUGLASS, Frederick Douglass. 96pp. 28499-9 $1.00

NARRATIVE OF SOJOURNER TRUTH, Sojourner Truth. 80pp. 29899-X $1.00

UP FROM SLAVERY, Booker T. Washington. 160pp. 28738-6 $2.00

A VINDICATION OF THE RIGHTS OF WOMAN, Mary Wollstonecraft. 224pp. 29036-0 $2.00

THE SUBJECTION OF WOMEN, John Stuart Mill. 112pp. 29601-6 $1.50

TAO TE CHING, Lao Tze. 112pp. 29792-6 $1.00

THE ANALECTS, Confucius. 128pp. 28484-0 $2.00

SELF-RELIANCE AND OTHER ESSAYS, Ralph Waldo Emerson. 128pp. 27790-9 $1.00

SELECTED ESSAYS, Michel de Montaigne. 96pp. 29109-X $1.50

DOVER · THRIFT · EDITIONS

NONFICTION

A MODEST PROPOSAL AND OTHER SATIRICAL WORKS, Jonathan Swift. 64pp. 28759-9 $1.00

UTOPIA, Sir Thomas More. 96pp. 29583-4 $1.50

THE AUTOBIOGRAPHY OF BENJAMIN FRANKLIN, Benjamin Franklin. 144pp. 29073-5 $1.50

COMMON SENSE, Thomas Paine. 64pp. 29602-4 $1.00

THE STORY OF MY LIFE, Helen Keller. 80pp. 29249-5 $1.00

GREAT SPEECHES, Abraham Lincoln. 112pp. 26872-1 $1.00

THE PRINCE, Niccolò Machiavelli. 80pp. 27274-5 $1.00

PRAGMATISM, William James. 128pp. 28270-8 $1.50

TOTEM AND TABOO, Sigmund Freud. 176pp. (Available in U.S. only) 40434-X $2.00

POETICS, Aristotle. 64pp. 29577-X $1.00

NICOMACHEAN ETHICS, Aristotle. 256pp. 40096-4 $2.00

MEDITATIONS, Marcus Aurelius. 128pp. 29823-X $1.50

SYMPOSIUM AND PHAEDRUS, Plato. 96pp. 27798-4 $1.50

THE TRIAL AND DEATH OF SOCRATES: Four Dialogues, Plato. 128pp. 27066-1 $1.00

THE BIRTH OF TRAGEDY, Friedrich Nietzsche. 96pp. 28515-4 $1.50

BEYOND GOOD AND EVIL: Prelude to a Philosophy of the Future, Friedrich Nietzsche. 176pp. 29868-X $1.50

CONFESSIONS OF AN ENGLISH OPIUM EATER, Thomas De Quincey. 80pp. 28742-4 $1.00

CIVIL DISOBEDIENCE AND OTHER ESSAYS, Henry David Thoreau. 96pp. 27563-9 $1.00

SELECTIONS FROM THE JOURNALS (Edited by Walter Harding), Herny David Thoreau. 96pp. 28760-2 $1.00

WALDEN; OR, LIFE IN THE WOODS, Henry David Thoreau. 224pp. 28495-6 $2.00

THE LAND OF LITTLE RAIN, Mary Austin. 96pp. 29037-9 $1.50

THE THEORY OF THE LEISURE CLASS, Thorstein Veblen. 256pp. 28062-4 $2.00

PLAYS

PROMETHEUS BOUND, Aeschylus. 64pp. 28762-9 $1.00

THE ORESTEIA TRILOGY: Agamemnon, The Libation-Bearers and The Furies, Aeschylus. 160pp. 29242-8 $1.50

LYSISTRATA, Aristophanes. 64pp. 28225-2 $1.00

WHAT EVERY WOMAN KNOWS, James Barrie. 80pp. (Available in U.S. only) 29578-8 $1.50

THE CHERRY ORCHARD, Anton Chekhov. 64pp. 26682-6 $1.00

THE THREE SISTERS, Anton Chekhov. 64pp. 27544-2 $1.00

UNCLE VANYA, Anton Chekhov. 64pp. 40159-6 $1.50

THE INSPECTOR GENERAL, Nikolai Gogol. 80pp. 28500-6 $1.50

THE WAY OF THE WORLD, William Congreve. 80pp. 27787-9 $1.50

BACCHAE, Euripides. 64pp. 29580-X $1.00

MEDEA, Euripides. 64pp. 27548-5 $1.00

THE MIKADO, William Schwenck Gilbert. 64pp. 27268-0 $1.50

FAUST, PART ONE, Johann Wolfgang von Goethe. 192pp. 28046-2 $2.00

SHE STOOPS TO CONQUER, Oliver Goldsmith. 80pp. 26867-5 $1.50

A DOLL'S HOUSE, Henrik Ibsen. 80pp. 27062-9 $1.00

HEDDA GABLER, Henrik Ibsen. 80pp. 26469-6 $1.50

GHOSTS, Henrik Ibsen. 64pp. 29852-3 $1.50

VOLPONE, Ben Jonson. 112pp. 28049-7 $1.50

DR. FAUSTUS, Christopher Marlowe. 64pp. 28208-2 $1.00

THE MISANTHROPE, Molière. 64pp. 27065-3 $1.00

DOVER · THRIFT · EDITIONS

PLAYS

THE EMPEROR JONES, Eugene O'Neill. 64pp. 29268-1 $1.50

BEYOND THE HORIZON, Eugene O'Neill. 96pp. 29085-9 $1.50

ANNA CHRISTIE, Eugene O'Neill. 80pp. 29985-6 $1.50

THE LONG VOYAGE HOME AND OTHER PLAYS, Eugene O'Neill. 80pp. 28755-6 $1.00

RIGHT YOU ARE, IF YOU THINK YOU ARE, Luigi Pirandello. 64pp. (Available in U.S. only) 29576-1 $1.50

SIX CHARACTERS IN SEARCH OF AN AUTHOR, Luigi Pirandello. 64pp. (Available in U.S. only) 29992-9 $1.50

HANDS AROUND, Arthur Schnitzler. 64pp. 28724-6 $1.00

ANTONY AND CLEOPATRA, William Shakespeare. 128pp. 40062-X $1.50

HAMLET, William Shakespeare. 128pp. 27278-8 $1.00

HENRY IV, William Shakespeare. 96pp. 29584-2 $1.00

RICHARD III, William Shakespeare. 112pp. 28747-5 $1.00

OTHELLO, William Shakespeare. 112pp. 29097-2 $1.00

JULIUS CAESAR, William Shakespeare. 80pp. 26876-4 $1.00

KING LEAR, William Shakespeare. 112pp. 28058-6 $1.00

MACBETH, William Shakespeare. 96pp. 27802-6 $1.00

THE MERCHANT OF VENICE, William Shakespeare. 96pp. 28492-1 $1.00

A MIDSUMMER NIGHT'S DREAM, William Shakespeare. 80pp. 27067-X $1.00

MUCH ADO ABOUT NOTHING, William Shakespeare. 80pp. 28272-4 $1.00

AS YOU LIKE IT, William Shakespeare. 80pp. 40432-3 $1.50

THE TAMING OF THE SHREW, William Shakespeare. 96pp. 29765-9 $1.00

TWELFTH NIGHT; OR, WHAT YOU WILL, William Shakespeare. 80pp. 29290-8 $1.00

ROMEO AND JULIET, William Shakespeare. 96pp. 27557-4 $1.00

ARMS AND THE MAN, George Bernard Shaw. 80pp. (Available in U.S. only) 26476-9 $1.50

PYGMALION, George Bernard Shaw. 96pp. (Available in U.S. only) 28222-8 $1.00

HEARTBREAK HOUSE, George Bernard Shaw. 128pp. (Available in U.S. only) 29291-6 $1.50

THE SCHOOL FOR SCANDAL, Richard Brinsley Sheridan. 96pp. 26687-7 $1.50

ANTIGONE, Sophocles. 64pp. 27804-2 $1.00

OEDIPUS REX, Sophocles. 64pp. 26877-2 $1.00

ELECTRA, Sophocles. 64pp. 28482-4 $1.00

MISS JULIE, August Strindberg. 64pp. 27281-8 $1.50

THE PLAYBOY OF THE WESTERN WORLD AND RIDERS TO THE SEA, J. M. Synge. 80pp. 27562-0 $1.50

THE IMPORTANCE OF BEING EARNEST, Oscar Wilde. 64pp. 26478-5 $1.00

LADY WINDERMERE'S FAN, Oscar Wilde. 64pp. 40078-6 $1.00

BOXED SETS

FIVE GREAT POETS: Poems by Shakespeare, Keats, Poe, Dickinson and Whitman, Dover. 416pp. 26942-6 $5.00

NINE GREAT POETS: Poems by Shakespeare, Keats, Blake, Coleridge, Wordsworth, Mrs. Browning, FitzGerald, Tennyson and Kipling, Dover. 704pp. 27633-3 $9.00

FIVE GREAT ENGLISH ROMANTIC POETS, Dover. 496pp. 27893-X $5.00

SEVEN GREAT ENGLISH VICTORIAN POETS: Seven Volumes, Dover. 592pp. 40204-5 $7.50

SIX GREAT AMERICAN POETS: Poems by Poe, Dickinson, Whitman, Longfellow, Frost and Millay, Dover. 512pp. (Available in U.S. only) 27425-X $6.00